B U T
N O W
I SEE

BUT NOW I SEE

ROSS PHILLIPS

CLAY BRIDGES PRESS

Amazing Grace!
How sweet the sound
That saved a wretch like me
I once was lost but now am found
Was blind but now I see.

—John Newton

To God,

Who saved a wretch like me.

1

HE WAS BORN IN the late summer of 1832, in a tiny cabin in rural southern Pennsylvania. In Europe, the French were taking steps forward in the study of the social sciences, and the British were taking steps backward in government reform. In America, Andrew Jackson was serving as president with an eye on reelection, and the US flag flying over the White House displayed twenty-four stars. Benjamin Bonneville led a wagon train across the Rockies through Wyoming for the first time. Cholera struck the northeastern seaboard, wiping out whole families including two cousins who lived in New York City.

In southern Pennsylvania, the summer had been warmer than usual, enough so that local farmers often remarked on it. The day of his birth was unusually hot with no breeze to speak of, and the cabin with its small windows was stifling. His mother, a pale and sickly woman in the best of times, lay on an old quilt on the rope frame bed in a stupor, the brutal exertion of labor pushing her to the edge of exhaustion. His father alternately stood over the bed breathing heavily with anxiety or paced around the cabin mopping his face with a handkerchief already soaked with sweat. The black wool coat he wore every day was draped over a chair, but he still wore a long-sleeved shirt, which clung to his thin frame in the heat. A doctor, a member of their congregation, was there. Also in attendance were two women from neighboring farms and family friends who had already shared much life together with them. One sat in a chair next to the bed and held his mother's hand silently, while the other wiped the sweat from his mother's face and sang hymns to her softly. For a long time, there was no other sound besides the cicadas in the trees outside.

Eventually, the birthing moved along, the doctor guiding the process with clipped instructions and sure hands, and he was born. One of the women washed him and swaddled him in a thin towel and placed him in his mother's arms. She was barely conscious by this time, yet she managed a tiny smile. His father walked outside into the hazy air, knelt in the dust, and raised his arms in silent praise for the miracle and blessing of the new life nestled on his wife's chest.

Thus, his life began. A few days later when his mother had recovered some of her strength, his father sat down with her at the kitchen table to discuss a name. It was not so much a discussion as a directive with which his mother complied, continuing a dynamic between them that had existed since their courting days. He would be Nathan Ezra Butterfield: Nathan after the Old Testament prophet who had called King David out in his sin and guided him in his leadership of Israel. His father had great hope and expectation that this boy, his own son, would become a great spiritual leader.

Many words could be used to describe Ezra Butterfield: deliberate, stern, self-assured, intelligent, devout. He always seemed to know what he was doing next and how, when, and why he was doing it. He had little humor in him, focusing instead mostly on the hard realities of life and the consequences of poor choices. He cared about others, but none who knew him considered him a man of compassion. He never seemed to question or doubt himself, and he genuinely did not care what others thought of him. He had excelled in every level of his schooling including seminary. He was a voracious reader. Intellectual pursuit was one of his highest ideals, and he had little time for those who thought otherwise. His faith in God was the main driving force of his life. He had answered an altar call given by his father during a revival meeting the summer he turned six, and he had never looked back. After completing seminary, he served in the mission field in Hawaii for a time, before accepting the call to be pastor of the small Lutheran church in Pennsylvania where he and his wife Mary had settled and started their family. He studied the Bible intently but rarely spoke or preached about grace. His expectations for his wife, his children, and himself were always high. Punishment for the children was usually swift and severe, and he did not hide his frustration with Mary when she made a mistake. He was not a cruel man, but he was emotionally distant.

Mary was the fourth of eleven children born to a quiet and loving mother and a forceful tyrant of a father. When she was four, she nearly died of scarlet fever, and she had been prone to sickness ever since. She was trained to follow orders from her father and older brothers, and this obedient tendency continued into young adulthood when she allowed Ezra— after he received grudging permission from her father—to direct their courtship and marriage. She loved Ezra in her way, but never from a clear sense of her own personhood. She merely saw herself as an extension of him, and he easily had enough force of will to keep her in his shadow.

The early years of Nathan's life were mostly uneventful. The world continued to move titanically forward, as in England's passage of the Slavery Abolition Act in 1833 under the charismatic leadership of William Wilberforce, but Nathan was blissfully unaware of that struggle. He spent his days playing with homemade toys in the kitchen while his mother prepared food and cleaned, and he often fell asleep watching his father studying the Bible and writing sermons by candlelight at the kitchen table, muttering to himself as he wrestled with a difficult passage in Hebrew or Greek.

When Nathan was three years old, his mother gave birth to his brother Joshua, so named by his father for the courageous leader of the Israelites who brought them into the land promised to them by God. The pregnancy and birth further taxed his mother's already slim reserves of energy. The doctor insisted that she be on bed rest for at least two weeks after the delivery, but even after that, she was wan and listless for months. Nathan was acutely aware of the change in her, and for periods of time, he was more fussy than usual in the way young children are when they sense their parents are struggling and less engaged. He loved her intensely and was worried about her but did not know what to do with his worry and felt unsettled. His father was of no comfort, distracted and occupied as he was with the many details of shepherding a congregation.

Nathan was completely unprepared to share his parents and household with another. At first, he was curious about this tiny being who seemed so helpless and innocent. As time went on, he became annoyed when the baby cried in the middle of the night and took much of his mother's attention during the day. But it was difficult to stay angry with the little one. He had such a calm and sunny disposition. His deep blue eyes sparkled when Nathan would entertain him at his mother's request. It did not seem to matter what silly game Nathan would invent. His brother would follow his every movement and giggle as though life could not be any better. They developed a close bond early on and spent many hours exploring the world around their cabin together.

Nathan and Joshua became good friends with the children who lived with their mother and grandparents on a neighboring farm. There were four boys named Matthew, Mark, Luke, and Timothy. No one ever got a satisfactory explanation from their father as to why he had not completed the Gospel set, and he died suddenly in a farming accident with the mystery still unsolved. The boys did not seem to care about this and got on with the business of being boys growing up in a farming community. Nathan became closest friends with Mark, and Joshua with Luke. There was also a younger sister named Hannah who became quite infatuated with Nathan. For his part, Nathan did not return her interest, but he treated her kindly, nevertheless.

When Nathan was six years old, his mother became pregnant again. The joy of this event turned to worry in the family as the pregnancy became more and more difficult and Mary took to her bed, often in great pain. One morning Nathan woke up to his father shouting for him to get the doctor. The sheets of their bed were drenched with blood and his mother was unresponsive. Nathan stared at the blood, which had started pooling on the floor, until his father slapped him in the face, shouting his name and pointing to the door. Nathan blinked and then turned and ran out, stopping only once on the way to the doctor's house to vomit. His mind raced with terrifying thoughts of his mother dying because he wasn't fast enough, and this spurred him on until the wind was rushing past his ears. He could barely speak when the doctor answered the door, but the grim look on the doctor's face told him the message had gotten through. The doctor's wife tried to persuade him to stay and rest, but he staggered outside in a panic. The doctor was just spurring his horse, and he rode after Nathan and hoisted him up in front of him. The short ride to the cabin seemed an eternity. When they reached it, his father was outside, speaking no words but gesturing wildly toward the cabin. It took only seconds for the doctor to assess the situation and he quickly got to work. The boys were shooed outside, but not before they heard the word *miscarriage*.

What followed was the longest day of Nathan's young life. He had no information to go on, only wild conjectures in his mind, the faint murmuring of his father and the doctor, and occasional moans from his mother. He was tasked with watching his brother, but his heart and attention were inside the cabin at his mother's side. He briefly played a hoop game with his brother but soon gave it up and sat on the door stoop, whittling a stick to a needle's point. Finally, as the sun was just disappearing through the trees, his father came outside followed by the doctor. The doctor patted Ezra on the shoulder, got on his horse without a word, and rode off. Ezra cleared his throat, looked up at the sky, then turned and looked at Nathan as if seeing him for the first time. Very quietly he said, "You boys should eat something." Then, almost as an afterthought, "The baby is dead. Your mother is resting." After several minutes of silence, he went back inside. Nathan was hit with such a wave of relief that he could hardly breathe. And then he began to cry. Joshua walked over and sat next to him. Slowly, he reached over and took Nathan's hand, and they sat there together until it became dark, and their father called them inside.

In the weeks that followed, Mary was like a ghost. She lay in bed for days, her skin white and waxen, hardly moving or making a sound. Finally, she accepted food and water and gained strength enough to get up and walk about the cabin. Her gait was slow and dreamlike. She would drift over to the empty cradle and hover there, then to a window where she would look out without seeing, then back to the cradle. She did no housework and cooked no meals. Women from the congregation came and cleaned and cooked and murmured to her soothingly. Ezra sat beside her and stroked her hair. Joshua drew pictures and left them at her feet. She registered nothing. Nathan kept his distance from her and was afraid as he had never been before, for it seemed his mother was lost to him.

Then one day she got up from her chair by the fireplace, walked to the cradle, carefully folded the blanket that was in it, and put it on a shelf with the other bedding; and she was back. She hugged the boys slowly and looked at Ezra with a tiny flutter of a smile. Each day she became a bit more animated, as though her spirit were slowly seeping back into her body from whatever dark place it had gone. She began very softly to talk to Ezra about having another baby. At first, he was gentle in saying no to her request. But as time went on and she became more and more insistent about this, it began to wear on his patience until one day he shouted at her that it was enough. She recoiled as if struck, then seemed to shrivel ever so slightly. From that day forward she wore a shawl of sadness about her thin shoulders.

The year 1840 saw more tragedy descend on the community. A ferociously hot summer led to turbulent weather late into the fall. One November day a winter storm suddenly blew in from the northeast, bringing with it blinding snow and sleet. A calf got loose from the neighboring farm and young Timothy, unbeknownst to his mother, went out to look for it, wearing only a thin denim coat. He became hopelessly lost out in the pasture, and by the time the family discovered he was missing and got a search party out, it was too late. They found calf and boy frozen to death, huddled together less than a hundred feet from the family home. Nathan would never forget the sight of the boy's mother on her knees at the grave site, pounding with her fists on the little mound of dirt; the sound of her high thin wail as women from the congregation gently yet firmly dragged her away from the grave, or the feel of Mark's shoulder, which was like wood, when Nathan awkwardly patted him on the way out of the tiny cemetery. Matthew stood like a statue, his chin quivering and his eyes swimming with tears but his shoulders squared, already assuming the mantle of the man of the family.

Shortly after the new year, Nathan came in from playing with Joshua and immediately sensed a tension in the air. His mother sat on the edge of the bed with a desperate smile on her face, her eyes fixed on Ezra. His father stood near the kitchen table. Nathan could see the taut muscles in his face as he clenched his jaw. Ezra opened his mouth twice as if to speak. His eyes narrowed as he glanced briefly at Mary, then with a little shake of his head, he turned and walked out of the cabin. Mary sat completely still for a few moments, then reached out her hand to Nathan. He walked toward her slowly and she took his hand. He could feel her trembling. She cleared her throat and said quietly, "Nathan, I am with child." He said nothing but studied her face. The smile that had been there slowly faded and she looked away. She sighed quietly and smoothed her dress, then gave his hand a gentle squeeze and got up and walked to the kitchen. Nathan watched her, sensing in her movements a mixture of joy and anxiety. In his own heart, he could feel dread growing, a hazy but unmistakable foreboding of tragedy lurking in the future. He squeezed his hands into fists and prayed that God would take the dark thoughts away and protect his mother.

In the months that followed, he kept a close eye on Mary. If she attempted to lift something heavy, he was there to help. If she seemed tired, he was the first to coax her to sit and rest. He did this out of great concern and love for her, but also because Ezra had almost nothing to do with her. His anger was a shimmering, pulsating barrier between them, never spoken but always present. Mary absorbed the punishment quietly, as she always did. Nathan was at first puzzled by his father's attitude, but his puzzlement turned to anger as the days went by and Ezra did not soften.

When the time came for the baby to be born, Ezra tersely commanded Nathan to summon the doctor. Mary was subdued and closed in on herself. Almost immediately things went wrong. When it was time to push Mary gave almost no effort, despite firm directives from the doctor. Ezra walked outside in disgust. Mary began to bleed and did not stop, and she slipped toward unconsciousness. The doctor at first tried smelling salts, then lightly slapped her face.

Somehow, he managed to deliver the baby, alive but slightly blue, and handed the girl to a neighbor woman who was present. When he turned back to Mary, his concern grew to alarm. He shouted her name and slapped her again, then yelled over his shoulder for Ezra. There was no color in Mary's face, her eyes were closed, and her mouth hung open. He yelled for Ezra again and checked for a pulse, but there was none. Ezra walked in with a frown that immediately disappeared when he saw the stricken look on the doctor's face. He stood frozen in the middle of the cabin, watching as if from a great distance while the doctor shook Mary by the shoulders, shouted her name, and checked once more for a pulse. After an eternity he gently closed her eyes, checked the time on his watch, and began packing up his bag. Nathan and Joshua came in and stopped just inside the door, their eyes wide. The baby began to cry, and the woman cooed softly to her, tears running down her cheeks. Joshua slowly stepped forward and grabbed the sleeve of his father's coat, looking up at him with eyes that pleaded for answers. Ezra did not move or speak. Nathan stepped back until the wall of the cabin stopped him. His eyes were locked on his mother's body. Her skin was translucent. Her hands lay with palms upward as if in a gesture of surrender. There was a look of absolute peace on her face.

The doctor finished packing up his instruments. He looked one last time at Mary, then at Ezra and the boys in turn. Each was frozen in place. With a sigh he turned and walked out of the cabin, wondering, as he had many times in his long career, how the family would navigate the shock and grief.

That night and for several days afterward, Nathan saw his father as he had never been before. Neighboring women talked to him as if he were a child, taking him by the hand and leading him to the table to eat. Men came and talked to him about church matters, and he did not look at them or speak. Nathan and Joshua helped him get dressed and undressed each day. He would not look at or touch the baby. Only gradually did Ezra begin to reengage with the world around him, but he was a shadow of himself. In his mind, he played over and over and over again the scene of his wife lying dead in the cabin. He too had noticed her posture of surrender and transcendent peace, and he came to believe that she had given up her life and given him a new life as a final gift, that he could perhaps turn from his anger and know joy. This thought came to him gently one night while he lay awake, and when it did his grief overwhelmed him, and he sobbed for hours, seeing with agonizing clarity for the first time how deeply Mary had loved him. He fell asleep with his arms stretched out to her side of the bed, whispering her name over and over.

When he woke in the morning light, he felt somehow emptied. He got up and took his daughter from the crib and called the boys to him. In their presence, he named the girl Rachael, a name in the Bible intimately connected with sorrow.

Nathan was lost for some time in his own world of grief. He was adrift and terrified, his anchor gone. He ached for the quiet, comforting presence of his mother. He did not feel he could turn to Ezra for comfort, accustomed as he was to his father's distance and still angry with him for the coldness shown to his mother. He had heard his father crying that night and his heart had softened a tiny fraction, but that was all.

Days blended into weeks and life went on. Ezra returned to his duties at the church. The boys went back to school in September. Neighboring farmers began to prepare for harvest. The leaves were turning in earnest when Ezra received a request from a clergyman friend of his in Charleston, South Carolina, to come and preach at his church. He accepted the invitation and decided to take Nathan with him. He saw this as an opportunity to further educate the boy on the evils of slavery. He had become involved in the abolitionist movement some twenty years previously, had met some former slaves and heard their grueling stories, and had seen the scars on their bodies. His righteous fury over the "peculiar institution" had grown with each year and he had spoken against it many times from the pulpit. Nathan was sometimes visited in his dreams by images of fire coming from his father's mouth and consuming a vast multitude of shrieking slave owners.

They took a coach, and as they traveled through the Blue Ridge Mountains, Ezra spoke to Nathan about this hideous stain on the nation. He told Nathan of people kidnapped from the African coast, crammed into ships, and cruelly shackled below decks, hundreds dying of disease and starvation on the long voyages north, dying in the sugarcane fields and oven fires of Cuba, finally brought to the shores of America to fuel the growing industry and agriculture of the young country. He told of the African slaves who had fought for their freedom and landed in Massachusetts on the Portuguese ship Amistad just the previous year; they had been freed after a legal battle that reached all the way to the federal Supreme Court, a remarkable case. As the coach descended into the lowlands nearer to Charleston, Ezra talked of the vast plantations of rice and cotton in the area harvested by tens of thousands of slaves, and the degrading and sometimes deadly living conditions they were forced to endure. His mouth twisted in bitterness as he spoke. "Imagine," he said, shaking his head slowly. "There are more black people than white in that city, and yet they are treated like animals. According to codes enacted two years ago by the state, they are not allowed to gather in groups, earn their own money, learn to read, grow their own crops, or own quality clothing." He leaned toward Nathan with fire in his eyes and said softly, "It is an abomination before Almighty God, and this country will pay dearly for it. Mark my words, boy." He sat back and said no more until they reached the city. Nathan sat quietly and looked out the coach window lost in his own thoughts. Occasionally, he would glance over at Ezra, and each time his father seemed to be sitting more rigidly, clenching the edges of his coat in his hands and muttering to himself.

Before the city even came into view, Nathan could smell the salt air, and his heart began to beat faster. He had never seen the ocean before, and he was fascinated by the thought of it. He had also never been to a large city. He was open-mouthed as they topped a rise and he saw the immense sprawl of buildings, and farther in the distance the masts of dozens of large ships lying at anchor. Ezra shouted up to the coachman to head for the harbor, then turned to Nathan and said quietly, "You need to see something, boy." Hearing his father's tone, Nathan knew better than to ask any questions about it. He sat back and watched as the city unfolded before him.

Never had he seen so many different kinds of people, all ages and in all manner of dress. Ezra tapped him with his walking stick more than once to keep him from staring. In a short time, they had made their way to within several blocks of the waterfront, and here they got out. Ezra briefly gave the coachman directions to wait, then gestured for Nathan to follow him. The smells of salt and fish and tar assaulted his nose as they walked.

As they got closer to the harbor, Nathan began to hear a man's voice carrying above the murmur of the crowded streets. He saw a large group of well-dressed men and women surrounding an enclosed space, and then a different smell came to him. It was faint at first, but it grew as they got closer to the gathering, and Nathan began to gag. It was a pungent mixture of sweat and human filth. As Nathan looked again at the crowd, he could see several people holding handkerchiefs to their noses. Then he saw the man who was speaking, a tall heavy figure with a bulbous nose. He was pointing to the space behind him, and Nathan looked in that direction. An area had been roped off roughly in the shape of a square, perhaps a hundred feet on each side, with a small opening on the side closest to the speaker. On the side farthest from him stood dozens of men and women and some children.

The females wore plain blouses and skirts; the males only trousers. All wore shackles around their necks and wrists and ankles.

Their skin glistened in the sun from fat that had been rubbed on them. There was a gorgeous rainbow of brown hues among them. Even from where he stood, Nathan could see the confusion and fear in their eyes. Close to the speaker was a small platform, and on it stood a tall and powerfully built African man. He stood erect and proud, looking directly at the crowd with a calmly disdainful expression. Next to him stood a shorter man, white, wearing grimy clothes and holding tightly to the chain attached to the other man's collar. As the man in front continued to speak the shorter man grinned and reached toward the African's mouth to show his teeth. The African jerked his head away, and immediately the shorter man cuffed him on the side of the head. The African drew himself up to his full height and looked down at the other man for a long moment, his eyes blazing, then said something in his native tongue and looked away. Nathan was spellbound.

He looked up at his father and saw a vein standing out on his forehead. His face was red and taut. As the man in front droned on, men in the crowd began to raise their hands and shout out bids. Eventually, a price was accepted, and the grimy man pulled on the chain of the slave to get him off the platform. The African did not move. The shorter man snarled something and yanked hard on the chain but the African stood his ground. The shorter man gestured to another man standing near the other slaves. This man ambled over to the platform and took out a revolver, cocking it and holding it to the head of the African. The crowd grew very quiet, except for the man who had won the bid for this slave and who now began yelling at the auctioneer. Almost a minute went by before the African slowly smiled and then stepped gracefully off the platform, trailing the grimy man behind him.

The auctioneer did not miss a beat but simply turned and surveyed the group of slaves behind him, then pointed to a young woman who was holding a baby. A third assistant walked over and reached for the baby. The woman shook her head and backed away. The man stepped forward and took hold of the baby, who began to cry. The woman screamed and lunged at the man, flailing at him with her manacled hands. The man with the revolver walked over and clubbed the woman in the head, and as she staggered back, he shot her in the stomach. The waterfront erupted into chaos. Africans were wailing and shouting, pulling at their chains. Gentlemen in the crowd were yelling, and shaking their fists at the auctioneer and his band of thugs. Ezra grabbed Nathan by his collar and began to drag him away as the crowd surged forward. The auctioneer blew several shrill blasts on a whistle that hung around his neck, and Nathan saw soldiers running from several directions toward the melee. When he looked back toward the Africans, all he could see was the man holding the baby, blackened teeth bared in a hideous grin.

Ezra and Nathan walked several blocks away from the waterfront before Ezra stopped on a street corner and turned Nathan to face him. Ezra's face was eerily calm. Though there were noises from the streets all around them, Nathan could hear his father's voice as he spoke softly and clearly. "Never forget what you have seen here today. Never. See and understand the evil that men do to each other." He stopped and looked into his son's eyes with burning intensity, then took Nathan by the arm and continued walking until they reached the place where they were to stay.

They remained in Charleston for a few days as Ezra completed his speaking engagement and visited some old friends. Nathan largely remained quiet for the rest of the trip, but always in his mind, the scenes from the waterfront played over and over in vivid detail, and his father's words haunted him.

They returned to Pennsylvania and settled into something of a routine, Ezra shepherding the church and the children attending to their schoolwork and chores around the home. Nathan found that he was a competent student but was bored with the work. The older man who served as a teacher in their country school was dull and unapproachable, and Nathan's mind often wandered.

A year after the trip to Charleston, two events occurred that would change the course of Nathan's life. The old teacher died, and a young man came to the community to take over teaching duties. His name was Mr. Oversby, a native of England, who had come to America a few years earlier over the strong objections of his wealthy parents. He was searching for adventure away from the stifling life of the aristocracy. When he ran out of money and his parents refused to send him more, he pursued a teaching certificate and eventually found his way to Pennsylvania. He was passionate about history, and it did not take long for Nathan to be captivated by his enthusiasm. While the other students played in the schoolyard during lunchtime, Nathan would sit in the schoolhouse and listen to Mr. Oversby's stories of the ancient Egyptian kings of Alexander and the Roman Empire and the Protestant Reformation. But there was more to Mr. Oversby than his knowledge of history. He had traveled widely, on his own and with his parents, and had much to tell about what he had seen in faraway lands. He had a keen mind and was well-informed about the social and political landscape in England. He was an engaging storyteller. Above all, he exuded compassion and encouragement. He quickly took an interest in Nathan. Often, Mr. Oversby would spend extra time with him at the end of a school day if he saw that Nathan was struggling with a particular subject. Nathan found himself beginning to confide in Mr. Oversby about his hopes and dreams, things he would never tell his father. Nathan invited him to supper at their home on many occasions, smiling to himself as Mr. Oversby firmly yet graciously held his own with Ezra as the old preacher plied him with deep theological questions.

Over the next few years, Nathan and Mr. Oversby developed a close bond. Watching the young man in front of the class day after day, Nathan found himself drawn to the idea of teaching. In his last year at the country school, Nathan began to talk with Mr. Oversby about pursuing this course. Mr. Oversby gave him some information on how to earn a teaching certificate and encouraged him to talk with Ezra about it. The thought of this conversation made Nathan's stomach tighten, but after a week of anxious hesitation, he finally screwed up his courage and approached his father with the idea. As he had anticipated, Ezra disapproved, at least initially. Though he was absolutely in favor of Nathan continuing his education, he much preferred that his son go to seminary and dedicate his life to ministry. But as they spoke Ezra detected a change in his son. Where before he would have been able to exert his will and influence Nathan's decisions, he now heard a resolve in his son's words and tone that had not been there before. He continued to play devil's advocate to Nathan's plans because that was his way, but inwardly he admired his son for standing up for what he wanted in his life. He knew that the young teacher had much to do with Nathan's current direction. As closed as Nathan could be when around his father, Ezra still saw the admiration Nathan had for Mr. Oversby whenever he spoke of him, and Ezra did not begrudge either Nathan or the teacher. Before the conversation was over, he decided to let Nathan follow his path. To Nathan, he said, "Give me some time to think on it. And pray about it. Seek God's will, son. That is the most important thing."

Nathan knew his father would end the conversation this way because Ezra said this same thing whenever they spoke of significant decisions. This was one indication to Nathan of his father's faith. He did not question his father's dedication to God, but he did question the depth of his faith. Whenever Ezra spoke of God and the spiritual journey, Nathan thought that something was missing. It was not necessarily a lack of passion or other emotion. Nathan had seen much of this in revival meetings, enough to know the difference between a charlatan and a contrite heart. It was more a lack of freedom, the absence of grace.

When Nathan read the books of the Old Testament, the teachings of Jesus, the letters of Paul, and the message of God's powerful and enduring love for a fallen people desperately in need of this kind of love rang clear and true. But it was not so when Ezra preached from the pulpit or even when he spoke alone with Nathan. As Nathan grew older, he realized that he could not rely on his father's faith to carry him, but still the lack of teaching on grace left a hole in him. This and the tragedies he had already experienced in his young life left him deeply skeptical. He felt he knew enough of Christian teachings to keep him in a solid place, and he could navigate his life from there. He began to make plans to go to a teacher's college, plans he knew would separate him from the life he knew, from his father. He knew this, and for the time being, he felt at peace.

2

BY THE TIME NATHAN neared the end of his seventeenth year, his future plans seemed to be nearly set. He had talked further with his father and had won his grudging support to become a teacher. The energetic and enterprising Mr. Oversby had applied for and received a one-year grant from the state for Nathan to be a pupil teacher at the school. Nathan had now been working alongside Mr. Oversby in the school for several months and found he loved it. The awkward transition from pupil to teacher in the same school had been navigated with skillful direction from Mr. Oversby. The work was long and difficult, but Nathan discovered he had an aptitude for putting together creative and challenging lesson plans and encouraging the students in their studies. Under his mentor's watchful eye, Nathan continued in this work and grew in knowledge and maturity. By the spring of 1852, he and Mr. Oversby agreed that he was ready to apply to a teacher's college.

His first choice was the Normal School in Albany, New York. Founded only two years before, it was already known as one of the top teacher's colleges in the country, and as yet there were no such colleges in Pennsylvania. With Mr. Oversby's help, he applied and was accepted, and so began a two-year process of rigorous study and training to earn his teacher's certificate.

Though he was greatly challenged in this work, he found again and again that Mr. Oversby had prepared him well, and his friend and mentor often sent him encouraging letters. Nathan also met several other students at the school who had a passion for teaching like himself. Most were around his age and from New York, but others were more nontraditional students and had viewpoints that led to spirited discussions in the dormitories after classes.

Nathan also began receiving letters from his brother, who had been accepted into the Lutheran seminary at Gettysburg and was eager to share what he was learning:

My dear Brother,

I hope you are well and attending to your studies. I am finding this new life quite stimulating and challenging at the same time. At present, there is spirited debate among the faculty regarding which language we should be studying in, German or American English, and also whether to put a greater emphasis on Lutheran distinctives such as the Confessions. I will spare you the details but suffice it to say that it is quite entertaining to see these stolid old men getting red in the face and puffing out their chests toward one another as they debate.

I am fascinated by the passions and intellects of some of the German theologians. It has quite enriched my reading of the Bible. My roommate is an energetic fellow from Boston who does not seem to hold back any opinion that comes to his mind. He is especially opposed to the Reformed theologians, believing Calvin to be an outright heretic. I have not yet formed an opinion on that line of theology, as I am rather more distracted in trying to accurately translate and understand complicated passages from the German commentaries.

The seminary itself is beautiful, situated on a small rise beyond the town. On especially fine evenings, some of my classmates and I like to sneak up to the cupola and enjoy a grand view of the area. I am told that though the seminary was founded only about thirty years ago, it already has a fine history, including being the first Lutheran seminary in the country to enroll a Black student.

Father seems to be doing fairly well at the homestead, continuing his shepherding of the church. A number of the older women in the congregation fuss over him quite a bit, so I believe he is well taken care of. Write to him, Nathan. I know he would appreciate hearing from you. So, would I.

Please know that I pray for you daily. I pray for your safety and health and provision, and for your studies. But more than that, I pray for your soul. I sense that over the years, you have drifted from God and that you are not at peace. I am concerned that you are relying too much on your own strength, morality, and wisdom as you walk your path, rather than relying on the Good Shepherd to guide you. I greatly encourage you to consider this, as I believe it to be of the utmost importance. I say this only out of love for you, brother.

Well, I shall close for now. Take care of yourself. I pray that God will bless and keep you in all that you do until we meet again.

With great affection, Joshua

***

Dear Joshua,

My apologies for not responding to you sooner. I can say with some honesty that I have been busy with my studies, which are taxing no doubt, but more than that I have struggled to know if and how to respond to your concern for me. After much thought, I have decided that it would most likely do me no harm to enter into a dialogue with you about this, though it causes me some discomfort. I believe that your intentions are good and that you are genuinely concerned for my welfare, so I am willing to walk this path with you, at least for a time.

To be honest, God has been little more than a distant thought to me for quite some time. I have taken your encouragement to heart and considered what has driven or guided me in my life, at least in recent years, and I find myself agreeing with you that I have mainly relied upon myself. It is difficult for me to know by what I should measure the relative success of my efforts thus far. If I compare myself to my classmates, I find that currently, I am doing fairly well. If I consider the picture I have in my mind of where I want to be at this time in my life, I would say the results are mixed. I do not know if God has plans for me, or if so how to discern them, or if I even care about this.

I do not say this flippantly. I have reflected on this much of late, again by your encouragement, and I find that I have not as of yet experienced God in my life in any meaningful way. I have seen great suffering and evil in my years so far, in my own life and in the lives of others, and therefore I am confronted with the age-old question of where God is in all of that. I also reflect on the example of Father—his harsh and unfeeling treatment of Mother and the absence of teaching or modeling grace to others. I do not understand how you experienced many of the same things I did, and how you could see God active and at work in any of it then or even now. I cannot trust or feel close to a God who let innocent Timothy and Mother die or who stands by while people live and die in brutal slavery. How do you answer these things, Joshua?

I realize that I have laid a heavy burden on you with this question. I do not expect you to solve this deep mystery for me, but I am certainly interested in your thoughts. I wish you well in your studies, and I look forward to hearing from you. And I will try to write to Father and Rachael.

Yours, Nathan

***

Dear Nathan,

I was thrilled to receive your letter. I will briefly say that there is little news of interest on my end. Studies continue apace, my classmates are entertaining and vexing by turns, the professors grumpy as usual. My only escape these days, other than walks through the countryside, is a delightful little bookstore in the town of Gettysburg where I can lose myself for hours. There is something about the feel and smell of books that is comforting to my soul.

The question that you posed in your letter has confounded theologians for millennia. Let me tell you right from the beginning that I do not know the answer, and I am glad to hear that you do not expect me to have it for you. The best I can do at this point is to share with you some of my thoughts about it so far. I believe that most people struggle with this question so much because there is no definitive answer. We are by our very nature driven to try to make sense of everything around us, and when we cannot do so, we become anxious and angry because it means there are forces at work beyond our control—forces that cause things to happen that seem unfair to us. We try to be objective and use our intellect to address something that is far beyond us, and our failure to resolve the dilemma draws us into deep and primitive fear that tends to drive us away from the things we do not understand. We are left with a choice: give in to that drive and try to live our lives within our finite understanding and resources, or surrender to the forces we do not understand, believing that these forces are ultimately benevolent and purposeful. Our decision profoundly affects how we perceive ourselves and others and the events in our lives, and how we use the resources available to us.

I choose to believe that there is a God who created all things, who is sovereign over all things, and who has a masterful plan for each thing He created, leading to ultimate perfection. I believe that mankind, starting with Adam and Eve, has tried to be like God and gain ultimate control over their circumstances, and this has caused immense pain and suffering through the ages. I believe evil does exist—because of pride, not because of God. I believe that no matter how much the twisted hearts and minds of mankind continue to cause pain and destruction, God's good plan will come to pass.

There is so much more to say on all of this, but I will leave that for future letters. Believe me, Nathan, I have struggled with this question too. It hurt me greatly to see how Father treated mother. I was broken over Timothy's death. I am saddened and enraged by slavery. I cannot explain to you adequately why I choose to believe, only that I am compelled by the beauty of the world around me, the love and kindness that I see enacted between others, and the promises of God when I read the Bible.

I pray that you will consider what I have said, and wrestle with it. I do not always have peace because of my choice to believe, but I have far more now than before I did, and I want that for you as well. God bless you, brother, and I look forward to hearing from you soon.

With affection, Joshua

———————

Dear Joshua,

Thank you for your last letter. I have indeed wrestled with the ideas you proposed, and I admit that I continue to have more questions than answers on these matters. I struggle to believe in something I cannot see or interact with, as I do with a flesh and blood person. How do I really know that God created the tree outside my dormitory window? What good can possibly come from slavery? Why should I believe what is written in the Bible?

I can respect your choice to believe in God and His goodness, but I do not know if I can go further than that. As for your assertion that mankind is driven to control their lives by the fear of the unknown, I find that an interesting idea but untenable. Is it not better to take action in one's life toward the end that one desires, rather than wait to see if an invisible Force will bring that good end to pass? I see that it does come down to an issue of faith, but at this time I choose to have faith in what I can experience with my senses, to use the brain I have to work things out. I know that I will not do a perfect job of this, but at least I know what I am dealing with.

As I read the words I just wrote, I am confronted with yet more evidence of the stubbornness I inherited from Father. Whether this will be a force for good or ill in my life remains to be seen. Nonetheless, I must bring an end to this letter now, as my studies are calling. Just a few months more and then I am hoping to be done with this section of my schooling. It has been good though exhausting. Best wishes to you, brother, until I hear from you again.

Yours, Nathan

***

It was now the late spring of 1854, and Nathan began to have conversations with his professors regarding placement in a school where he could begin his teaching career in earnest. After several options were considered, it was decided that he would go to the newly formed territory of Kansas, where there was a shortage of teachers.

Nathan's feelings about this placement were decidedly mixed. He was certainly excited and curious to begin teaching in his own classroom, but the area to which he was going was quickly becoming a hotbed of sectional unrest. The line between slave and free states set out by the Missouri Compromise of 1820 had been erased earlier in 1854 by the Kansas/Nebraska Act, which in essence gave the citizens of the territory the power to decide whether they would uphold slavery or not. Emotions on both sides of the issue were already running high when Nathan arrived in the town of Lecompton in the eastern part of the territory at the beginning of the summer. Though he was sickened to overhear conversations in the streets about Blacks being akin to apes and good for nothing except hard labor, he decided to keep his head down and focus on what he was there to do. He found a small place to rent on the outskirts of town, drew up his lesson plans, and prepared himself to begin the school year. Over the next several months, he slipped into a comfortable routine and distanced himself the best he could from the rising tension around him.

Joshua was faithful in writing to him. His brother had graduated from seminary shortly before Nathan moved to Kansas territory and traveled to England to work with mentally ill and indigent people under the guidance of Dorothea Dix, a powerful American reformer and advocate for those populations. But after several months, Joshua felt called to return to the States and work in the hospital for the mentally ill in Harrisburg, Pennsylvania, that Dix had helped to establish a few years earlier. His letters burst with passion as he described the horrid conditions of many government institutions in America and Great Britain where such people were sometimes treated worse than animals in many cases. His letters also remarked on the momentum that was built to ensure more humane treatment for the mentally ill:

> Brother, it is a shock to me to see how, in this day and age, people
> who are suffering through no fault of their own are treated with

such contempt and lack of compassion. My mind turns, time and again to the example of Christ healing the sick and demon-possessed, spending time in the company of lepers and other poor and outcast members of society, loving them simply and profoundly because they were made in His image. I can only hope to aspire to a tiny fraction of that kind of love as I work with these dear people. That is in some measure how I can respond to the wretchedness and evil and suffering that I am confronted with in this world. From the work of Ms. Dix and others, I gather, hope and encouragement that kindness and justice will ultimately win out. I would rather hang onto this and be thought a fool than resign myself to despair and do nothing.

Nathan could only shake his head as he read his brother's words. He continued to be jaundiced toward the thought of any real goodness or fairness in the world. This position was

strengthened by daily evidence in the territory: the hate-filled rhetoric from pro-slavery orators on the street corners of Lecompton, fistfights between slavers and free-staters, and the growing reports of deadly violence in outlying areas. He could not understand his brother's blind choice to look past the ugliness of humanity and do good anyway. He was not angry at Joshua for this. To the contrary, he felt a grudging admiration for him. Regardless of circumstance, his brother seemed guided by an unswerving moral compass.

In the late spring of 1856, two significant events occurred. The first, which had profound effects on the region and indeed the nation, took place not far from Lecompton. Nathan woke one bright morning to angry shouting in the street outside his room. He hurriedly dressed and went downstairs and was informed by other boarders at the breakfast table that several pro-slavery citizens had been murdered by a company of abolitionists led by John Brown just outside Lawrence in response to several stores and homes being destroyed in Lawrence by a pro-slavery contingent just days before. Emotions at the table were electric with talk of people arming themselves to join Brown's company, preparing to defend their homes and businesses, or leaving the territory altogether. Amidst the heated conversations, Nathan quickly and quietly ate his breakfast and excused himself. With the school year recently completed, he needed time to himself to think. The region was tearing itself apart, and he did not know whether to stay and weather the storm or leave and start a new chapter in his life.

The decision was more or less made for him with the second significant event, heralded by a letter from Joshua he received the next day. Ezra had suffered a serious stroke and could barely move or talk. He was being well looked after by members of the congregation. The doctor was not at all sure about his prognosis. Joshua and Rachael were there and urged Nathan to come. Nathan sent a hurried letter stating that he would get there as soon as he could. A fellow teacher suggested that the quickest route home would be on horseback to St. Louis, then the railroad from there. Nathan bought a horse and tack and a revolver from a farrier in town. He packed a few basic supplies and a change of clothes, said hurried goodbyes to the few friends he had made in town, and left on a rainy morning at the end of May.

His initial fears about attacks from Indians faded as the days went by. The few Indians he saw were usually at a great distance and only seemed interested in their own affairs. Mostly, he had a great deal of time to think. Uppermost in his mind was the state of his father. Ezra had always had a robust constitution; his iron will seemed to fuel his body to brush aside even widespread illnesses that passed through the region. His illness was a shock to Nathan who, up to this point, had viewed Ezra as an indomitable force of nature. He now was faced with the reality of his father's frailty and even mortality, and it brought up in Nathan an unexpected mix of terror and relief—terror that he could no longer count on Ezra to be the absolute bedrock upon which Nathan could build his own life, and relief that he now had permission to be frail himself. He did of course wonder how Ezra would be - whether he would be able to talk or think as he used to and whether his personality would be different.

He thought about his brother and sister, particularly their decisions to put a pause on their own lives to care for Ezra. Joshua had done well at the hospital in Harrisburg and now holds an administrative position, though his great compassion for the patients continued to drive him to engage in direct care whenever he could. He sounded exhausted but happy in his letters, and Nathan was glad for him.

Rachael had been working as a live-in governess for a wealthy family in Pittsburgh for several years when she received the news about Ezra. She had always kept in close contact with him even after she moved to the city for her governess position, and she did not give a second thought to putting in her notice and moving back to the cabin as soon as she possibly could. In many ways, she took after Mary, particularly in her pale complexion and quiet demeanor. She had a few friends but kept mostly to herself. A few men from Pittsburgh had attempted to court her, but she had little interest in marriage, at least for now. There always seemed to be a pall of sadness over her, though she did not generally have much to be sad about. It was as though she had at some level decided to identify with her namesake. However, she was not sickly as her mother had been, and there was enough spirit in her to do bold things such as moving on her own to a large city. Though Nathan worried about her from time to time, he always had the sense that she could look after herself.

He thought also about his own future. His teaching experience in Lecompton had been positive and rewarding in some ways, but the rising ugliness in the region made him uneasy to return. Even if he wanted to, he did not know what the future held given his father's situation. It could be a short stay to make sure Ezra would be all right and had the help he needed, or it could be much more than that. Perhaps Nathan could find a teaching position in the area. He decided that for now there were too many unknowns and that trying to discern future events and plans was a waste of time.

After several days of hard riding, he reached St. Louis, and he summoned enough energy to navigate the noise and bustle of the great city to sell the horse and tack, find a hotel for the night, and buy a train ticket for Harrisburg. He had a quick supper and turned in early, but though he was exhausted from riding, he did not sleep well, unsettled as he was by the recent disruptions in his life and an uncertain future before him.

The train ride was generally uneventful but seemed interminable, marked by frequent stops for fuel and passengers and switches to other lines. Besides the occasional quiet conversation between a few of the passengers, most kept to themselves, which suited Nathan. He tried to sleep but found it nearly impossible to get in a comfortable position or slow his mind. In the brief periods he was able to doze, he had disjointed dreams of his family and often woke with a stiff neck and a headache. By the time he arrived at Harrisburg on a lazy Tuesday afternoon, he was irritable and restless. His brother met him at the station with a smile and a fierce hug, and they were soon on their way to the cabin in a wagon borrowed from a neighbor. As they rode Joshua filled him in on his father's condition, which was generally stable, and news of the community, which did not interest Nathan.

As the sun was setting, they pulled into the yard in front of the cabin and came to a stop. For a few moments, there was quiet except for mourning doves calling to each other. Nathan noticed that the cabin had been fixed up in some places and that brush around it had been trimmed, and he remarked on this. Joshua told him that members of the congregation had generously given their time over the last several months as a gesture of love and appreciation for Ezra. Joshua once again was grateful for these simple and gracious people who cared for his father so fiercely.

The door of the cabin opened, and Rachael stepped out and walked toward them. Nathan was struck by the beautiful young woman she had become. Her hair was pinned up in the back showing her long, slender neck. She wore a simple dress and an apron which was wrinkled and stained, but still, she seemed stately. She moved with easy grace. Nathan jumped down from the wagon and came toward her. She gave him a tired smile and reached out her arms. "It's good to see you, brother."

He gave her a squeeze. "You too, sis. How are you?"

"Pretty well, I would say. Father has been asking after you." She took his arm, and they walked slowly toward the cabin. Nathan looked back at Joshua, who smiled and waved him away.

"Don't worry, brother. I'll handle things here. Father is more important."

When they walked into the cabin, it took a few moments for Nathan's eyes to adjust. The curtains were drawn, and other than a candle on a nightstand near his father's bed and another on the kitchen table, it was dark. Nathan looked at Rachael. "Is he sleeping?"

"I don't think so. He was talking with me just a few minutes ago."

Ezra gave a gravelly cough and cleared his throat. "Come here, boy."

Nathan walked slowly to the bed. Ezra reached out a hand and took one of Nathan's. The feel of his father's hand told Nathan much. It was extremely thin and cold, yet there was strength there. Ezra's face told a similar story. His cheekbones and eye sockets were almost skeletal, an uneven stubble barely covering taut skin webbed with tiny blue veins. But when he opened his eyes and fixed his gaze on Nathan, a glimmer of the old spark was there, a sure sign that the old man was not done yet. He took a few deep breaths to gather his strength and regarded his son.

"How was your trip?" He slurred a bit as he spoke, and Nathan could sense the frustration as his father closed his eyes briefly and gave a small sigh. Clear and strong speech had been a honed skill and a matter of pride for Ezra.

Nathan shrugged. "Long."

"How was Kansas Territory when you left?"

"A mess."

Ezra frowned slightly. "That all you've got to say on the matter?"

"People are angry about the massacre." For some reason, Nathan felt shy in his father's presence. He shifted his weight from one foot to the other and looked out the window. Joshua entered the cabin and closed the door.

Ezra said, "Your brother is not a man of many words."

Joshua smiled at him and Nathan. "Yes, he did not exactly talk my ear off on the way from the station."

"Hmmph." Ezra adjusted his head and looked at Nathan.

"I'm sorry, Father. I'm just tired from traveling."

"Well, bring a chair over and stretch your legs out, and tell me more about what's been happening with you."

Nathan did so and they spent the next hour or so becoming reacquainted. Darkness fell as Rachael prepared supper. Joshua lit two more candles and pulled up a chair next to Nathan, but he mostly listened to the conversation between the other two. Ezra spoke slowly and softly but his mind was sharp. As Nathan began to relax, he talked more about the strife he had left behind, and Ezra listened closely and asked penetrating questions. To Nathan's surprise, his father seemed particularly interested in Nathan's own thoughts and feelings about current events, and Nathan found himself on uncertain ground. He was relieved when Ezra turned the conversation to Nathan's teaching experiences. Ezra also showed keen interest in this and even offered some resources he had used in his sermon preparations. For the first time in years, Nathan felt something more than a distant respect for his father, experiencing as he was that night a softening in Ezra.

Rachael brought plates of food for them all, and they sat around their father's bed, talking and laughing over childhood stories. Ezra needed help occasionally to bring food to his mouth and wipe his face, which Rachael tended to do with practiced skill. He was mostly quiet during the meal, watching his children with a twinkle in his eye. As time wore on his eyelids drooped and he began to nod. Rachael set about preparing him for bed while Joshua took the dishes into the kitchen and began to wash up. Nathan stepped outside onto the small porch and leaned against a railing, breathing in the night air.

After some time Rachael came out and sat on the top stair. Nathan sat beside her, and she leaned into him. "Sometimes, I feel like the work is never done."

He put his arm around her. "I can't begin to imagine. Thanks for all you've done for him."

"He misses you, you know." She turned to look at Nathan. "He may not have come out and said it, but it's true."

Nathan sighed. "I've missed him, too. Missed all of you, really."

"Why didn't you write more?"

"I got busy getting my own life started."

"It doesn't take that long to write a letter, Nathan."

He smiled at her and tucked a stray lock of hair behind her ear. "Well, I guess I need to do better in that department, don't I?"

"Yes, you do." She gently nudged him on the shoulder and returned his smile. "So how is Father doing, really?"

"Overall, I believe he's on the mend." Rachael rubbed her forehead wearily on her sleeve. "He's stubborn, you know that, so sometimes he is not the best patient."

"Will his speech improve? Will he be able to walk again?"

"The doctor is cautiously optimistic that he will recover most of his faculties over time. But honestly, nobody knows for certain."

Nathan looked out at the yard and was quiet for a moment. "He seems different somehow. Not as hard."

"That could be the stroke, or maybe he sees life differently now. Who knows?"

Nathan sighed deeply, then turned to Rachael. "And how are you doing, sister?"

"Oh, now there is a question." She paused. "I am not really sure. Some days, I miss my life in Pittsburgh. I had a good friend I could talk to when I needed to, and I enjoyed my church. It was exciting to experience a big city after growing up here. But there were times I was lonely and missed our family. The family I worked for was mostly kind to me, though the mother could be quite overbearing at times." She stretched her legs out and continued. "I knew when I received the news about Father that coming here to care for him was the right thing to do, and in some ways, it is fulfilling for me."

"But?"

She sighed. "But I don't know what direction to go from here. When Father can be on his own, I am not sure whether I want to return to Pittsburgh and resume my life there, settle here and find work, or start a whole new chapter somewhere else."

"Rachael, what is your heart drawn to?"

Rachael was very still for a moment, then sat up straight and looked Nathan in the eye. "I want to write."

"Tell me more."

"Oh, Nathan, there is so much in me that wants to come out!" Rachael's eyes shown as she spoke. "I know that I have been very quiet all these years, but my mind and my heart are alive with deep thoughts and feelings, and I want to explore them and express them! When I read of Susanna Moodie's adventures settling in

Canada, I feel my soul drawn to the wild frontier. When I am in one of Fanny Fern's books and she writes of the experiences of the ordinary woman, it seems as though she is speaking directly to me. It is so easy for me to be swept up in the grand romance of Jane Austen or the Bronte sisters, to be stirred by the quiet beauty of Elizabeth Barrett Browning's poetry, to—"

Nathan laughed and held up his hands in surrender. "All right, all right, you've sold me! You have the soul and passion of a writer. So, will you pursue it?"

"I would love to, Nathan. I know that I may not make much money at it, although a few women like Harriet Beecher Stowe have done quite well, and I know it is not a direction for women that is supported by society—goodness, you should read Nathaniel Hawthorne going on about women writers disrupting his income! But the more I think about it, the more I want to give it a try."

"Then I think you should."

"Do you really think so? Oh, Nathan!" She hugged him tightly. "You don't know how much it means to me for you to support me in this. I wasn't sure how you or Joshua or Father would take it. You are the first one I've told."

"I have a feeling that Joshua will support you. Father, I imagine, will be the tougher sell." "Yes, I think you're right."

"So, the life of a wife and mother is not for you, eh?"

Rachael shook her head. "Not now. Maybe not ever. I have seen that life close up—the ridiculous strutting and courting rituals, marriages arranged for the gain of money and power, and the way women are trapped and treated like possessions and objects to be used. I want nothing to do with that."

"But surely there is a chance for true love someday?"

"So far, the men who have pursued me are pompous fools who think far more of themselves than they should. I don't have much hope that a good and humble man will come along any time soon and capture my heart."

"No Mr. Darcy or Heathcliff?"

She laughed and gave him a playful shove. "You are a rat, Nathan Butterfield!"

They talked on into the night as the moon rose and set behind the trees. Nathan treasured this time and did not want it to end, but eventually, his eyes grew heavy, and he kissed his sister on her forehead and went to bed.

In the days and weeks that followed, the family settled into a pleasant if predictable routine. The siblings divided tasks between them to care for Ezra and the cabin and the grounds. Nathan rode into town for food and other things they needed once a week. He spent time talking with his father during the day, and with

Joshua and Rachael in the evenings after chores were done. Ezra slowly regained strength and mobility under the watchful eye of Rachael and the doctor and members of the congregation.

Eventually, Nathan's thoughts began to turn more toward his own future. His love of teaching had not dimmed in his time away, and letters from his colleagues in the Kansas Territory assured him that there would be a job waiting for him should he decide to return. He was occasionally offered jobs by townspeople who owned various factories in the area, but these did not appeal to him. And similar to Rachael, he was not drawn to a life of marriage and family at this time. Several young women in town and at church would catch his eye and smile at him, and Rachael mercilessly teased him about their attention. Well-meaning fathers invited him to their homes for supper to meet their daughters, but Nathan always politely declined. His spirit was restless, and he did not want to be tamed by domestic life.

Events in the country continued to stir his emotions and his imagination as well. The plight of slaves had been of keen interest to him ever since his ghastly boyhood experience at the Charleston docks with his father. He did not consider himself an abolitionist, but he was gripped by the intense struggle of a people to gain their freedom. He had read of the slave revolts by Nat Turner and others when he was a boy, and now in the spring of 1857, another powerful tale splashed across the newspaper pages, that of Dred Scott and his family. A titanic legal battle had raged between the Scotts and their various owners for over ten years, and it had finally reached the federal Supreme Court. In May Nathan read with some disbelief how Justice Roger Taney had cast the deciding vote against the family being free. The most wrenching of the justice's dissenting points to Nathan was his assertion that people of African descent were not considered US citizens and therefore did not have the right to even bring a case to the court.

This development brought the abolitionists howling once more onto the public stage. When he went to town, he heard the strident voices on the street corners preaching against the evil and injustice just perpetrated and the need to take action, and his mind returned to the streets of Lecompton, where only a year ago, where the cries for justice had come from precisely the opposite side. The difference in this situation was that only a short time later, all was made right as the Scott's new owner set them free, and the abolitionists once again sang praises to a just and merciful God.

Slowly, Nathan's path became clear to him as spring gave way to summer. Ezra was now walking, although gingerly, and able to dress himself and prepare simple meals. The doctor gained assurances from church members that they would continue to help Ezra as much as he needed. Rachael gathered the courage to share her dream of writing with Joshua and Ezra and found to her surprise that her father was the more supportive of the two, though Joshua had only minor concerns about her future. She learned of a women's writing group in New York and made plans to move there and join them in the fall. Joshua, more confident now in his father's progress and ongoing support, decided to resume his duties at the hospital full-time. All of this gave Nathan a sense that he was no longer a necessary presence in Pennsylvania, and he yearned to teach again. Though he knew he would miss the conversations with Rachael and Joshua and even his father, the quiet times on the porch in the gentle evening light, and the good-natured spirit of the townspeople, he also knew that he needed to follow his passion. Having come to this clarity in his mind, he wrote to a colleague in Lecompton and secured his old teaching position there, and made arrangements to move back to Kansas Territory by the end of July.

The days flew by swiftly, and suddenly it was the morning of his leaving. Nathan rose while it was still dark and checked that everything was packed as it should be. Rachael was already up and making breakfast. He walked into the kitchen and poured himself a cup of coffee and touched her on the shoulder. She turned to him, and he could see that she had been crying. He put his arm around her waist and gave her a brief smile. "You've started already?"

She wiped her eyes on her sleeve. "You know me; I always want to get a jump on things. Now sit down at the table, and I'll bring you some food."

Joshua came in and hung his hat on a peg by the door. "The wagon's ready to go." He inhaled deeply. "Bless you, Rachael; the coffee and food smell divine." He walked over and sat down opposite Nathan. His hair was plastered to his head except for a cowlick at the back; his eyes were red and puffy, and there was a shadow of whiskers on his face. Nathan looked at him and smiled.

"What?"

"Nothing, you're just a vision of loveliness this morning."

"Well, it's not my fault that you chose to leave at the very crack of dawn."

Rachael giggled as she carried plates of food to the table. Joshua feigned outrage and pointed at her. "And you are not helping any."

Nathan snorted. "Leave the girl alone. At least she's not sleeping the day away like some people I know."

They continued to banter as they ate, and soon enough the meal was done, and it was time to go. Ezra had been sleeping during this time but now as Nathan carried his baggage to the wagon, Rachael woke him, and he slowly dressed. As Nathan finished loading the wagon, Ezra came out, walking with a cane while Rachael held his free arm. Nathan turned and walked to his father. They looked each other in the eyes for a long moment before Nathan stepped forward and embraced him. "It has been good to spend time with you, Father. Take care of yourself."

"God go with you, son. I will pray every day that He will keep you safe and well until we meet again."

Nathan moved to Rachael, who was weeping softly. "Oh, sister, more tears."

He held her tightly and she whispered, "Nathan, I will miss you so."

After a moment he released her and stepped back. "I wish you the best with your writing. Be sure to tell me how it is going."

He mounted the wagon beside Joshua, gave a wave to his father and sister, and they moved off. When he looked back, he could just see in the grey dawn light Rachael turning back toward the cabin, and the white of Ezra's shirt as he stood like a statue looking toward the wagon.

The ride to the train station was uneventful and quiet. Neither Nathan nor Joshua seemed in the mood to talk. Just before Nathan boarded the train, he and Joshua hugged and Joshua said, "God bless you, brother. Keep in touch." Then he was gone.

The journey back to Lecompton was long and marked by heat and thunderstorms much of the way. Interested in watching the weather even as a boy, Nathan marveled at the towering cloud formations and magnificent displays of lightning over the prairies. One afternoon on the train just outside St. Louis, he witnessed a small tornado a few miles off, its sinuous grey column snaking down and briefly touching the open grassland in an explosion of dirt and debris before ascending back to the dry line.

He reached the town on a warm and blustery afternoon, left his belongings at the small room he was to let, and walked to a nearby inn where he met a teacher friend. Over bottles of beer, they caught up with each other, and the warmth of his friend's company was comforting evidence to Nathan that his choice to return to this place seemed to be a good one.

Over the next several weeks, he gathered materials and sketched out lesson plans. He met the new head schoolmaster for the area, a welcome change from the austere and egotistical man who had supervised Nathan in his previous term. The new man was much more progressive and gave Nathan great freedom to teach in his own unique style. Nathan was grateful for this and felt excitement for the coming year.

It did not take him long to settle back into life in Lecompton. The school year started fairly smoothly, though Nathan found it necessary to exercise a firm hand with several of the boys in his class who thought it funny to challenge his authority in front of the other students. These boys quickly learned that Nathan would not tolerate such behavior, though, in the end, he won them over more through humor and fairness than iron discipline.

Life outside of teaching was rather quiet but satisfying, nonetheless. Nathan picked up where he had left off with his friends in town, and they often gathered in the evenings at one inn or another and debated teaching theories and classroom structure over supper. A few new teachers had come to the area while Nathan was away, and they proved to be welcome additions to the circle of colleagues. Nathan also looked forward to letters from his family, which came at regular intervals. He learned that Joshua was heading up a collaborative effort among hospitals in the east, and as usual, his excitement about the work fairly leaped off the pages.

Rachael was enjoying her writing group and finding much to keep her busy in New York. In one of her letters, she made brief mention of a certain young man who had begun calling on her.

Nathan smiled as he recalled her comments to him about dating during one of their conversations at the cabin, which now seemed long ago. He even received some letters from his father. Though it was at times difficult to make out words from the shaky script, Nathan gleaned that things at the church and in town were moving on apace. His father seemed to have regained much of his clarity and vigor, for which Nathan was glad.

A pleasant fall gave way to a sudden and bitter winter. Some days it snowed so hard that Nathan had no choice but to cancel school for the safety of his students. He spent these days helping others shovel out of their homes and take care of livestock, and even on occasion joined in a snowball fight with children in town. He was grateful when townspeople invited him to their homes for supper on cold nights, and he treasured quiet walks home on clear nights with the stars to keep him company.

At long last, the harsh prairie winter loosened its grip and milder weather returned. Snowdrops and tulips began to poke their heads out in some of the yards in town. The streets as usual became a quagmire, and Nathan joined a small army of townspeople in sluicing water off the main roads and laying split logs to corduroy where they could. Eventually, the sun did its work as well and dried the mud and clay, making easier passage for man and horse and wagon.

Tragically, the gentle weather in the spring of 1858 did not translate into more peaceful relations in the region. The anger between pro-slavers and free-staters, which had simmered over the winter, erupted once more into deadly violence not far from Lecompton, in a place called Marais de Cygnes. This time, the violence was led by a force of pro-slavery radicals, resulting in several deaths.

Once again arguments and fistfights broke out in the town's streets, and Nathan's bitterness over the conflict grew. When anyone asked his position on the matter, he invariably maintained a tight-lipped silence, not trusting himself to filter the words that swirled in his mind.

Months passed, and another school term began uneventfully. News from Pennsylvania continued to flow from his family: Joshua receiving official recognition from the governor for his work in the hospital, Rachael becoming more serious about the young man mentioned in previous letters, and his father's church beginning to support the missionary work of Hudson Taylor in China. As the holidays approached, Nathan made plans to visit his family, but another harsh winter put an end to that, and Nathan instead spent Christmas with a colleague and his young family just outside of town. Though Nathan longed to be with his own family, especially at this time of year, he forgot his homesickness when he walked in the door of his friend's home and was greeted with a kiss on the cheek and a cup of hot cider from his friend's wife and a shy smile from their three-year-old son. He would remember the warmth and kindness shown to him that day for many years to come.

Once more, winter gave way to spring. Nathan was pleased with the progress of his students and told them so whenever he could. At last, the term came to an end, and Nathan looked forward to a pleasant and relaxing summer, with a visit to Pennsylvania planned for July. But fate intervened yet again when he received a letter from Joshua early in June stating that his father had suffered another stroke, this one so serious that Ezra was unconscious for nearly a week. It was not clear whether he would survive. Nathan made all possible speed in getting to Pennsylvania, every mile dreading the possibility that he would be greeted upon his arrival with the news that his father was dead. After what seemed an eternity, his train pulled into Harrisburg, and his brother was waiting for him with the report that Ezra had regained consciousness and was making efforts to communicate. The relief that washed over Nathan had a tranquilizing effect, and he slept on the ride home, curled up in a horse blanket in the back of the wagon.

A somber mood hung over the cabin when he went in to see his father. Rachael sat at the kitchen table staring into space, dark circles under her eyes. Nathan put a hand on her shoulder, and she continued to stare, but reached up a hand to cover his and gave it a gentle squeeze. He walked over to the bed and was unsettled by what he saw. The left side of Ezra's face was almost completely slack. His eyelids drooped nearly to the point of closing. His mouth hung open and a thin string of drool glistened on his chin. He made no sign of recognition or even acknowledgment when Nathan put a hand on his arm. Nathan paused a moment and looked at his father, then turned to walk away.

"Talk to him." Rachael's voice, though very quiet, startled him. "I think it helps him to hear our voices."

"I don't know what to say."

"I'm not sure it matters."

Nathan stood in awkward silence, then sighed and turned back to his father. "Hello, Father." He paused, at a loss for words. Ezra's right hand stirred slightly, and his fingers fluttered as if brushing away a fly. Nathan leaned forward. "It is good to see you."

Rachael shifted in her chair. "He comes and goes. Sometimes, I read to him, and he seems to be listening intently, and other times he seems locked away in his mind."

"What does the doctor say?"

"He does not know if Father will regain any of his faculties, stay as he is, or die soon. He does not offer me any assurances."

Nathan rubbed a hand over his face. "Well, I can't blame him. There is so little anyone knows about these things."

"So, you don't offer me assurances either?" There was a hard edge to Rachael's voice.

"Rachael, what do you want me to say? Everything will be fine? That it is in God's hands?"

She sighed. "I am sorry, Nathan. I am exhausted and scared and confused, and it is frustrating that I can do nothing for him, that we do not have answers. Even so, it does not give me the right to speak to you so."

"No harm done. I imagine none of us will be on our best behavior in the days ahead." He held out a hand to her. "Come, I think you could use some fresh air."

Rachael gave him a tired smile and took his hand, and together they walked out and sat on the porch. Joshua joined them and they sat in silence for a while. Eventually, they began to talk quietly about what lay ahead with their father, and after a time, with nothing settled, they realized they were hungry and went in to make supper.

And so as they had done before, the three settled into a routine of caring for their father and the cabin and talking together in the evenings. The days came and went, neighbors and church members stopped in to help and spend time at the bedside, and Ezra remained much as he was. They did what they could, and they waited.

3

AS THE LEAVES BEGAN to turn in the fall of 1859, Ezra made almost imperceptible progress. He began to move the fingers of his left hand a bit more, then his left arm. His eyes became brighter. Eventually, with help, he could sit up in his bed and move his head from side to side. He could neither speak nor write, and his children could see the frustration in his eyes, the deep yearning to communicate, which was so much a part of his nature. They learned to pay more attention to the expressiveness of his eyes, and from this, they were able to more or less understand what he wanted to convey. His spirit seemed intact and even his dignity, though it was sorely tried on the numerous occasions when he soiled himself and needed to be cleaned up. He bore these and other humiliations with patience and grace, and his caregivers were grateful for it.

Though things at the cabin seemed peaceful, in the country it was not so. The Wyandotte Constitution was passed in Kansas in early October abolishing slavery and setting off a fresh wave of unrest in that region. Not two weeks later, John Brown, leader of the Pottawatomie Massacre in Kansas just four years previously, attempted to lead a slave revolt by seizing control of the Federal arsenal in Harpers Ferry, Virginia. Robert E. Lee sent J. E. B. Stuart with a contingent of Marines to deal with the uprising, crushing it in two days, but the shock waves from this incident were felt around the country. Some of Brown's followers were killed or imprisoned during and after the attempted raid, and Brown himself was hanged in early December. For this, he became a martyr and a saint for the abolitionist cause.

Yet there was cause for celebration in the Butterfield family. Christian Taylor, who had been courting Rachael for over two years, finally worked up the nerve to approach Ezra and ask for the old man's permission to marry her. Ezra listened with patient restraint while the young man zealously stumbled and stuttered his way through an explanation of his feelings for Rachael and how he planned to provide for her. Ezra had seen Christian's qualities over time in his frequent visits to the cabin and believed that he had the makings of a good husband. When the young man finally brought his presentation to a close, Ezra looked kindly into his eyes and placed a hand on his arm, and slowly nodded. On Christmas Day Christian took a knee and proposed to Rachael sweetly and simply, and in her tears was the answer he had so fervently hoped for. At dinner, Nathan and Joshua offered hearty congratulations and listened patiently as their sister brimmed over with ideas for the wedding. A date was set for the following spring.

The wedding was held at the church in town, and the congregation lovingly outdid themselves in bringing the simple building to life inside and out with flowers from their own gardens. Though it was a rather cold and windy day, the church was well-warmed by an old wood stove and the good wishes of people who had known and loved the family for so many years. The service was performed by a young minister from a neighboring town who had been mentored by Ezra. The old man sat hunched in a wheelchair at the front of the sanctuary and his shining eyes missed nothing. Nathan walked his sister down the aisle, and there was hardly a dry eye in the church when she stopped in front of Ezra and kissed him gently on the forehead before continuing to the altar. In the gentle glow of candlelight, Nathan saw his sister's lovely face glowing of its own accord, as she looked into the eyes of the man she loved and pledged her life to him.

The young couple settled into a small home on the outskirts of town and began creating their new life together. Christian was a lawyer with a sharp mind and a voracious work ethic, and it was not long before he had a burgeoning practice. Rachael busied herself with turning their house into a home. She had help from friends in town but showed a keen talent for decorating all on her own and took care to be frugal.

The two often came to the cabin for supper, and it was during these times that Nathan became acquainted with Christian's fervent vision for a united nation. As the family sat around the table he talked on and on with fire in his eyes about the growing dissent in the southern states and the potential danger that represented. Rachael would lay a hand on his arm and smile apologetically at her family, but her husband talked on. He especially mentioned a fellow attorney and aspiring politician from Illinois named Abraham Lincoln, who appeared to be a rising star in the young Republican party. Christian held this man in high regard and believed that Lincoln had the quiet strength and moral conviction to keep the nation together. He heard from a colleague that Lincoln was scheduled to speak in a small town outside Pittsburgh just before the Republican convention, and he urged Nathan and Joshua to go with him and listen to the man. Joshua graciously declined, citing work obligations, but Nathan was curious and agreed to accompany Christian and Rachael. He had heard of Lincoln from various news sources but had not paid much attention to him until now.

They arrived in Pittsburgh at the end of April on a warm and windy day. Rachael, not sharing her husband's passion for politics, was spending the day with friends in the city. Nathan and Christian took a carriage from their hotel to the town where Lincoln would be speaking. They walked toward a gathering crowd and found a place to stand near a raised platform. An older man was orating in a strong, clear voice about the shining merits of the Republican party.

Christian leaned over to Nathan. "That's George Wilson, the new mayor of Pittsburgh. A lot of hot air, but his heart is in the right place." Nathan smiled but his attention remained on the platform. The old man finished his remarks and gestured behind him, and from a row of seated dignitaries at the back of the stage rose a tall, gaunt figure. Though his posture was somewhat stooped, he still towered over Wilson as he approached the lectern, and his tall stovepipe hat added to the illusion of enormous height. He fumbled in a vest pocket and took out a watch on a fob, opened the watch and glanced at the time, then leaned casually on the lectern and made a quiet remark to the audience. A scattering of laughter followed. Nathan noticed that as soon as Lincoln began to speak the crowd quieted and leaned forward.

Over the next fifteen minutes, the tall man spoke about the state of the nation and the hopes of the Republican party to repair and strengthen it. His voice was gentle and higher in tone than Nathan had expected. His speech was plain and unassuming, often salted with colloquial stories that suggested a simple rural upbringing. But his message was clear and compelling, and Nathan found himself thinking, "This is a man I could follow." Lincoln finished his speech and turned to resume his seat, but Wilson rushed up and grabbed his arm, and brought him forward to the edge of the stage while the crowd applauded. Lincoln seemed clearly uncomfortable with this attention and stood awkwardly, managing a craggy smile.

Christian nudged Nathan's shoulder, and they turned to go. On the way home Christian chattered excitedly about the possibility of Lincoln being nominated for president, and Nathan made some effort to engage, but the words of the tall figure on the stage echoed in his mind.

Little of note occurred in the Butterfield family over the next several months, but as the fall approached, they could sense the tension rising in the nation. The newspapers kept a wary eye on the southern states and reported ever-increasing vitriol coming from southern congressmen regarding the trampling of states' rights, which they foresaw if Lincoln were elected. When November came and Lincoln was indeed voted into the White House, overcoming a somewhat confused Democratic ticket, the southern vitriol increased. The word *secession* began to be spoken more frequently in state houses across the lower states, much to the dismay and anger of most in the north. Christian was of course delighted with Lincoln's election, but even he saw a potential crisis looming for the country.

Less than a week before Christmas, the fears of many were realized, as the congress of South Carolina voted to secede from the Union. Several other southern houses began similar proceedings and by the time the bells rang in the new year of 1861, talk in many states north and south turned to the prospect of military mobilization. The situation rapidly grew worse when a supply ship bound for Fort Sumter in Charleston Harbor was fired upon by batteries from other forts ringing the harbor. The nation stepped closer to the precipice of war.

As the days passed, Nathan watched his father struggle to make even tiny gains toward better functioning. He could swallow better now, but he could barely move his arms and needed help even to turn in his bed. Joshua was busier than ever in his work with the hospitals and could only visit the cabin occasionally. Christian's law practice was now booming, and Rachael was expecting their first child. Nathan saw that his future lay in caring full-time for Ezra, and he set his mind to the task. The dear people of the congregation continued to help where they could, and he was grateful for it.

A welcome source of support came from the neighbors he had known as a boy. Matthew, Mark, and Luke had remained in the area over the years to help their mother with the farm. She had become a shadow of her former self after the death of her youngest boy and had difficulty handling much beyond simple daily tasks. All three boys had grown into sturdy men, hard workers who loved the land and spent what little leisure time they had hunting, pursuing women, and drinking a lot of beer. Though subtle differences made each man unique, together they were a loud, cheerful, brawling bunch who could never fail to bring a smile to Nathan's face. They descended on the cabin one night soon after he had returned from the west and picked up as though he had never left, laughing and retelling stories of their childhood together and punching each other for no apparent reason. They had visited at least once a week since then, and they always left Nathan in a better mood. With Ezra, they were gentle and respectful for the most part, but their bawdy humor at times spilled out into the room. The crooked smile on his face confirmed his abiding love for these boys, nonetheless. What Nathan did not expect was the relationship that began to grow between these men and Christian. When they first met one evening at the cabin, Nathan thought that the significant difference in their backgrounds and lifestyles would lead to awkwardness at best. Indeed, for the first few minutes, all were fairly reserved. But when Christian began to talk with restrained bitterness about the lengthening list of seceding southern states, the brothers leaned forward and gave a rousing chorus of support for his views, and an unlikely bond was formed.

Whenever Christian and Rachael visited and the boys were there, the conversation inevitably turned to the prospect of war between the states, and Nathan watched Rachael's face become etched with worry.

In the early morning hours of April 12, 1861, the nation fell over the precipice. The batteries surrounding Fort Sumter in Charleston Harbor began a devastating barrage, which lasted more than a day, causing significant damage to the structure itself. After minimal efforts to return fire, Major Robert Anderson soon saw the futility of further resistance and raised a white flag over the ramparts. Ironically, the first casualties of the war were not incurred during the bombardment but rather during a planned 100-gun salute at the surrender of the fort, in which an unexpected cannon explosion killed one southern soldier and wounded another. But the most significant casualty of that engagement was peace.

The next time Nathan saw his brother-in-law, which was at dinner in their home in late April, Christian was beside himself. He paced the living room floor and heaped curses on the southern troops and Jefferson Davis, recently elected president of the provisional government of the Confederacy. He applauded Lincoln's call for 75,000 volunteers to put down this ridiculous rebellion, and when Rachael quietly expressed concern for the safety of the men answering the call, Christian scoffed at her and labeled them patriots in defense of a just cause. With fire in her eyes, she squared her shoulders and opened her mouth, but Nathan stepped between them and suggested that she finish preparations for the meal. She turned on her heel and stalked away to the kitchen. Nathan gave Christian a sharp look and jerked his head in Rachael's direction.

Christian sighed and deflated a bit. He walked to the kitchen and put a hand on Rachael's shoulder and muttered an apology. She barely acknowledged the gesture, and the rest of the evening was ruled by palpable tension.

Matthew, Mark, and Luke were changed. Now when they visited the cabin, they were less jovial. They talked of the war, for such it was now being declared, with an edge in their voices. They watched friends and neighbors signing up to join Lincoln's army, and they nodded with grim approval. They read to Nathan from the local newspaper of Lee and McClellan tangling in the wooded mountains of western Virginia and began to talk of enlisting themselves. When news reached the town of the debacle at Bull Run in late July—the inept leadership of McDowell, the overconfidence of Union troops melting before Jackson's solid stand and the fiery exuberance of his brigade, and the panicky retreat to the capital—the die was cast. Early one morning in August, the three brothers showed up at the cabin with muskets tied to their saddle bags and blankets slung over their shoulders. They were off to join a company of volunteer infantry that was forming in the area. When Nathan asked what was to become of the farm, they said that on their urging, their mother had decided to sell it and move north to live with relatives. Nathan nodded slowly and looked at them, noting how grown up they seemed as they sat up straight and proud in their saddles, but also seeing their boyishness just beneath the surface.

He shook hands with each of them in turn, but before they turned to go, Mark looked him once more in the eyes and said, "Nathan, will you come with us?"

"I can't, Mark. Father needs me."

Mark opened his mouth to speak again, but Matthew held up his hand and then looked kindly at Nathan. "Yes, he does, and you are a good son." Then a mischievous grin played over his face. "But if you ever tire of this life and are looking for some adventure, come find us. I'm sure we could find room in a tent for you somewhere. But for God's sake practice your aim. You never could hit a damn thing." And with that, he turned his horse to the path and set off at a trot. Nathan smiled and gave a final wave as the other two followed their brother, and he watched them until they rounded a turn and were out of sight.

That evening Christian and Rachael came for dinner. Rachael was due very soon and was clearly uncomfortable, but she put a brave face on and was full of lively chatter during the meal. Christian was uncharacteristically quiet, and Ezra from his bed watched him intently. After they finished eating and Rachael was cleaning up in the kitchen, Christian asked Nathan to join him out on the porch. They sat side by side in silence for some time, watching the shadows lengthen across the yard. Finally Christian cleared his throat.

"I've decided to enlist."

Nathan closed his eyes and sighed, then looked at Christian. "This is not the time."

"I'm not going tomorrow. I know I need to be here for the birth of my child."

"And what about after that?"

"Rachael and the baby can stay with her cousins in Pittsburgh."

"Have you talked this through with her?"

Christian was quiet for a moment. "No."

"What in God's name are you thinking?" Nathan surprised himself with the intensity of his response. "You have responsibilities here! Your place is here! You are a husband and a father, and they need you. Be a man!"

"And what kind of man would I be if I did not stand up for what is right?"

Nathan stood abruptly and faced Christian. "This is not your fight. This is a political squabble that will end soon enough."

Now Christian stood. "This is **every** man's fight! Do you not believe in freedom and equality for all?"

"I do."

"As do I. And I choose to step forward and be counted with those who will end tyranny and oppression of others and see justice done, by force of arms if necessary. What will you choose?"

Before Nathan could answer, Christian stepped toward the cabin door. Impulsively Nathan reached out and grabbed his arm. Christian turned to him, breathing heavily. Nathan said quietly, "Please talk to Rachael soon."

Christian gave a small nod. "I will."

Nathan lay in his bed that night with Christian's words echoing in his mind. He was still angry at the prospect of the man leaving his wife and baby to fend for themselves, while he went off on a foolhardy crusade that could very easily end his life. And yet the message was there, quietly insisting that he pay attention to it. "What will you choose?" Images of the Charleston docks flooded his mind, and he was sickened all over again. What did he believe in his heart? Were all men actually created equal, born with the unalienable right to life, liberty, and the pursuit of happiness? If so, could he stand by and watch as millions were treated like animals to support the economy of others? Could he do that and live his life with a clear conscience? He was not a soldier, that was clear. He did not know the hardships and privations of military life. He could not picture himself aiming a musket at another man with the intent to kill or standing in the face of enemy fire. And yet. And yet.

In due time Rachael gave birth to a beautiful boy, and they named him Micah, after the steadfast Old Testament prophet. When Nathan went to visit them soon after the birth, he knew without being told that Christian had talked with Rachael about his plan to enlist. Her smile when Nathan entered their house was thin and strained, and Christian rarely looked in her direction. Nathan made a good effort to cheerfully engage with them, even holding the baby for a short time though he felt awkward doing so. After a short while, he excused himself on the pretense of business in town and took his leave. He did not envy Christian the experience of facing his sister's anger and disappointment, though certainly, she had every right to feel these things.

The days passed. The heat of summer gave way to the mellow warmth of autumn, and the trees surrounding the cabin began to turn. On a crisp October morning, Christian visited the cabin with a quiet and earnest air about him. He exchanged pleasantries with Ezra and then motioned Nathan to step outside. Nathan knew at once what was to come. Once they were on the porch and the door was closed, Christian turned to him and said, "I am going to enlist tomorrow."

"Are you sure?"

"My mind is made up."

"Are Rachael and the baby provided for?"

"Yes."

"Will you tell my father?"

"Yes, but I wanted to tell you first."

Nathan looked out at the trees in the yard and watched a hawk circling lazily in the air. Then he turned to Christian and said, "So be it."

Christian took a step toward him. "Nathan, come with me."

"No."

"Please. It is the right thing to do."

"Maybe for you."

Christian shook his head. "I wish I could respect your decision, but I cannot."

"I can live with that."

"I hope you can." Christian reached out his hand. "Take care of yourself, Nathan. Until we meet again."

Nathan took his hand in a firm grasp and looked Christian in the eye. "Whatever you do, come back to your family alive. They need you."

"I will do all I can toward that goal." Christian stepped off the porch and mounted his horse. Before he turned the horse toward the path, he said quietly, "If you change your mind, you can meet me at the farrier's in town at eight a. m. Think about it." With a final nod to Nathan, he rode off.

The night was long. Nathan could not fall asleep; his mind kept going over and over the exchange with Christian. Finally, he slept, and he had a dream. He stood on a hill overlooking a vast plain. In the middle of the plain were an enormous furnace, belching flame, and dark smoke. A long column of Black people, men and women, and children were chained together in a line leading to the furnace. Men with evil grinning faces were pulling the line toward the furnace and throwing the Black people in one at a time. The screams of the dying reached his ears. The end of the line was quite close to him, and the man at the end strained toward him and shouted, "Please, sir! Help us! You can save us!" Nathan stood and looked down at him and did nothing. The man shouted again, "Please, sir, won't you do something to help us? What will you choose?" Suddenly Nathan found himself chained up in the line, being dragged inexorably toward the furnace, closer and closer. The heat became unbearable; his skin began to crackle and turn black, and he heard himself screaming in agony and fear.

He woke with a start, his throat tight and sweat streaming down his face. It took several minutes for his breathing to slow. He got out of bed, his body shaking. He walked to the window and saw the first faint light of dawn coming through the trees. Eventually, his heart calmed, his mind cleared, and he quietly began to pack for his journey.

4

THE TWO RODE QUIETLY side by side in the soft morning light. It was unusually warm for October and their coats were rolled up and tied to their packs.
They followed the road that led out of town, with scrub pine and tall grass and
farmland for scenery. They were headed for an encampment about twenty miles
distant, a company of volunteer infantry forming from towns around the area, part
of the newest infantry regiment from Pennsylvania. Nathan thought it possible
that Matthew, Mark, and Luke had joined this company. He wondered what they
would think when he rode into camp.

He thought of Ezra much of the way. He had never been comfortable saying
goodbye. His solution in this case was to write the old man a letter. After starting
four times and not finding the right words to explain his decision, he ended up
with a short scribble, apologizing for the abrupt departure and promising to do his
best to visit as much as possible. He knew it fell far short of how he should have
taken leave from his father, but he told himself that it was all he could manage at
the time.

After riding at a clipped pace for a couple of hours, they topped a low rise and
saw the encampment spread out before them. The sound of a ragged musket volley
reached them, accompanied by a cloud of smoke carried away on a slight breeze.
Tents were lined up in neat rows, and overall, the camp gave a solid impression
of order and discipline. The two men rode on and came to the edge of the camp,

ringed by a split rail fence. Near a gap in the fence, a man sat on a rude bench. He was dressed almost entirely in black from his coat to his boots, except for a white collar around his neck. His hat lay on the ground next to him, and he was engrossed in a book on his lap. As Nathan and Christian approached, he looked up, closed the book, and stood, his hand raised in greeting. He was quite tall, with a ruddy complexion and a pleasant smile.

"Good day to you, gentlemen, and God bless you." He spoke with a fairly strong Scandinavian accent.

The two men reined in and looked at each other for a moment. Finally, Nathan leaned forward and said, "Good day to you, sir. We are here to enlist."

The smile grew wider. "Well, we are grateful for your courage and willingness to serve. I am Chaplain Ericcson, the spiritual shepherd of this company. Please follow me, and I will show you to the recruiting sergeant. He will be pleased to see new men." He turned and began walking toward a large wall tent, and Nathan and Christian followed on horseback. At the tent, they dismounted and tethered their horses, then entered the tent behind the chaplain. A sergeant sat at a simple desk poring over papers. He looked up as the men entered. The chaplain stepped forward, and the sergeant saluted him. "What can I do for you, Chaplain?"

"New men here to enlist, Sergeant. I trust you will treat them well." Ericcson shook hands with both men and walked out. The sergeant took a blank sheet of paper from a stack on the desk, dunked a nib pen in an inkwell, and said in a bored voice, "Names?"

Each stated his name, and the sergeant scratched out a quick note, then folded it and held it out to Nathan. "Take this to the medical tent and give it to the orderly. The tent's near the back of the camp, there's a sign on it. The surgeon will do an examination to see if you are fit for service."

Nathan took the note and asked, "What do we do with our horses?"

"You can talk with the quartermaster about the army buying them from you."

"But—"

"Good day, gentlemen. I have a lot of work to do." The sergeant had already turned his attention back to the sheaf of papers on his desk.

Christian looked at Nathan and shrugged. They walked out and led the horses by their bridles down a wide path lined with simple white tents, two canvas pieces buttoned together and held up by rough wooden poles and rope. Before they had gotten far, a column of soldiers turned onto the path headed straight for them, led by a small sergeant with a walrus mustache. As the column approached, he pointed at the two men and barked, "Step aside! This is the company street!"

Nathan and Christian did their best to get themselves and the horses off to one side. As the column marched past, the sergeant glared at them, then growled at the company to halt. The two men hurried on sheepishly, looking for the medical tent. Eventually, they found it and once again tethered their horses. An orderly wearing sack coat and sky-blue trousers lounged on a camp chair at the entrance to the tent. "Can I help you, gentlemen?"

Nathan stepped forward and handed him the note. The orderly scanned it briefly and looked at them. "Wait here." He stepped into the tent and reappeared a minute later, gesturing for the two men to enter. Once inside they met the surgeon, a tall man with close-cropped hair and eyeglasses that lent him a serious air. He ordered them to strip down to their undergarments and proceeded with a brief examination. He looked briefly at their overall musculature, had them show him their teeth, told them to stand on one foot and then bend over, looked at their hands and feet, and asked them a few cursory questions about their histories of diseases and accidents. He pronounced them fit for service and filled out a form for each of them and then told them to get dressed.

"Keep these forms with you, the first sergeant will need to see them. Head over to the quartermaster store, the big wall tent to my right, and he will get you accoutered. Welcome to Company D, gentlemen."

Once dressed, Nathan and Christian walked out and followed in the direction the orderly pointed with their horses in tow. They soon arrived at the quartermaster store and were each quickly issued the following items: a forage cap, four-button wool sack coat, wool trousers with canvas suspenders, boots, two pairs of cotton socks, haversack, leather belt, and brass buckle, cap pouch, a cartridge box with shoulder strap, bayonet scabbard, rubberized poncho, blanket, tin cup, set of flatware, small fry pan, and a knapsack. They did their best to pack the equipment for carrying. The quartermaster sergeant asked if they wanted to sell their horses to the government, and they said they did. He walked outside with them and briefly examined the horses, quoted the two men a flat rate, which they accepted, and the deal was done. Upon re-entering the tent, Christian pointed at muskets packed in long wooden boxes in one corner. "What about those?"

The sergeant gave him a wry smile. "You'll get them later. First, you need to report to the first sergeant, and he'll get you situated." He gave them directions to the first sergeant's tent, then began making notes in a logbook. The two men sighed, picked up their equipment, and walked back in the direction of the company street.

They stopped at the first wall tent on the street as they had been directed and put their packs on the ground. They stood for a moment, unsure of what to do. Finally, Christian said, "Hello?"

One of the tent flaps was pushed aside and out walked the small sergeant they had seen earlier. He looked at each of them and his eyes narrowed. "I remember you two, walking down the company street like a couple of blind mules. What do you want?"

Nathan cleared his throat. "We've, uh, enlisted, and we were told by the quartermaster to report to you."

The sergeant coolly eyed their packs, then fixed his stare back on them. "I see. Did you get a form from the surgeon?"

They handed the papers to him, and he glanced at them. He looked up and saw a corporal standing by a tent across the way, shouting to him and gesturing for him to walk over. He looked back to the two men in front of him. "I'm First Sergeant Jeremiah. Corporal Purvill will show you where to place your equipment on the company street; then you'll go to the quartermaster tent and get some shelter halves and rope. The corporal can help you scrounge up some poles and stakes." He consulted a watch on a fob. "Get your tent set up, put on your uniforms, and stow your equipment. Mess is at five p.m. Dismissed." Christian began a half-hearted salute and the sergeant held up a hand. "No, you do not salute me. I am a non-commissioned officer. A simple 'Yes, sergeant' will do." With that, he walked back into his tent.

The corporal, a thin and somewhat nervous-looking man, led them to an open space at the end of the row of tents, and they left their equipment there. They were issued two shelter halves and some rope from the quartermaster. Corporal Purvill showed them how to affix the rope and use whittled branches for ridge and support poles and stakes so that when they were finished, they had a low, sturdy A-frame that would keep off rain and sun. The corporal sighed. "I wish we had hay to sleep on, but for now, you'll just have to make do. Remember, mess is at five."

Nathan asked, "Corporal, do you know if three brothers enlisted in this company about two months ago? Last name of Tollefson?"

Purvill thought a moment, then shook his head. "No. They may be in one of the other companies." He gave a quick nod and walked off.

They took off their civilian coats and pants and put on their uniforms, which were surprisingly comfortable though ill-fitting. They looked at each other and smiled. Then Christian chuckled. Nathan could not help himself and joined in, and soon both were roaring with laughter. Soldiers walking by gave them curious glances and shook their heads. A man poked his head out of the shelter next to them with an annoyed look on his face.

"Hey, you two jokers! Keep it down. I'm tryin' to get some sleep over here."

Christian caught his breath and waved to him. "Sorry, friend. We're just getting used to these fine clothes."

The man's face grew red. He heaved himself out of the tent and onto his feet. He was well over six feet tall and built like a bear. He strode over to Christian and stopped inches from him, his fists clenched. "Listen, Hayseed. You're obviously new here, so I'm going to fill you in on a couple things. First off, I am not your friend. Second, this "fine clothing" may not look like much, but it's good enough to fight in, and die for our country. My brother was killed in the fighting in western Virginia two months ago. He was proud to wear this uniform, and by God, you'd better be too."

Christian took a step back and stammered, "I'm sorry, I meant no— "

"Stow it! Just stop acting like a jackass and have some respect for the men in this army and what we're here to do." With that the man spun on his heels and stalked off, muttering to himself.

Nathan stepped toward Christian, whose face was drained of color, and lightly punched him in the shoulder. "I think you just made a friend."

Christian slowly let out his breath and gave Nathan a wry smile. "I may have just wet myself."

They laughed and turned to the business of putting their blankets and other equipment in the shelter.

At five o'clock they put their kitchenware in their haversacks and followed a trail of men heading for the mess tent. Every body type and personality imaginable surrounded them. Some men joked and laughed with each other, some were engrossed in serious conversation, and some shuffled through the line silently with their eyes on the ground. When it was their turn, Nathan and Christian held out their pans and were given a ladle of simple stew, some cooked carrots, and a biscuit each. They filled their cups from a water barrel and sat on a patch of grass. As they started to eat, a large shadow blocked the sun in front of them. They looked up and there stood the man from the shelter next to them, his face impassive. He looked directly at Christian.

"Seems we got off on the wrong foot. I just got a hard letter from home, and I was not in a good frame of mind. I'm sorry for coming at you the way I did." He held out a massive hand. "Judah Bylszacek. Most people call me Billy. It's easier."

Christian reached up and took his hand, surprised at the gentle grip. "Christian Taylor. And no need to apologize. I can rub people the wrong way sometimes." He pointed to the grass next to them. "Care to join us?"

"Thanks, I will." He carefully set his food and water on the ground and sat, surprisingly nimble for a man of his size. The group ate in silence for a minute before he looked at Nathan and spoke. "I don't know your name."

"Nathan Butterfield."

"Where are you boys from?"

"A small town about twenty miles east of here. How about you?"

"I have a farm about five miles from here. My brother and I worked it together." Christian shifted uncomfortably. "I am so sorry that I—"

Billy waved him off. "That's done. His death wasn't your fault. I can grieve without being an ass." And with that, he began to share with them the details of life in the company.

He proved quite patient with their questions and had a wry sense of humor. They learned that the captain (Shields) was a cynical and exacting man but a good commander in the field and that First Sergeant Jeremiah was hard but fair. After they finished eating, they quickly washed their dishes in a bucket of water outside the mess tent and then walked together back to their shelters. Billy showed them how to put on the belts holding the cartridge box and cap pouch and bayonet scabbard, and he was beginning to teach them to stand at attention and at ease when Corporal Purvill approached them.

"You new men fall in with me. Bring your canteens. We'll be doing some light drilling." He had Nathan stand at his right shoulder and Christian about two feet behind Nathan; then he gave the order to march, and they made their way just beyond the camp to an open field, where perhaps a dozen other men were sitting or standing in the grass.

Sergeant Jeremiah was there, talking with another sergeant in low tones, and when he saw the men approaching, he nodded to the sergeant and faced the group. In a forceful tone, he barked, "Fall in!"

The men looked at each other in some confusion, and Corporal Purvill and the other sergeant began to push and pull them until they were in two lines facing Sergeant Jeremiah. When the men were more or less set, the other sergeant nodded to Jeremiah, walked around the two lines, and stood behind them. Corporal Purvill took a position at the far right of the front line. Jeremiah cleared his throat.

"You men are mostly new to military life. That will change quickly. It is the job of myself and the other noncommissioned officers of this company to form you into an efficient fighting unit as part of the Army of the Potomac. There is a lot to learn. Listen carefully, use your brains, and watch the more experienced men, and you'll catch on. Choose to be lazy or try any funny business and I promise you that things will not go well for you."

A tall man wearing spectacles in the second line spoke up. "What do you mean by—"

"Quiet in the ranks!" Jeremiah glared the man into submission. "This is not question and answer time." He addressed the group. "Believe me when I say that it is in your best interest to learn to obey orders as soon as possible. Learn to work as a unit, and it will save some lives." He stopped for a moment. "Notice I did not say 'every life.' Some of you will die. That is war.

Make peace with that in your own way. Now, let's begin."

For the next hour and a half, Jeremiah drilled the squad. He ran them through the proper way to fall in, to size up and count off, to stand at attention. He explained the structure and use of file partners and ranks. He had them left face and right face, in which the two ranks transformed into a column of fours, then back to company front. He marched them through the field with the sergeant and corporal shouting at them to watch their dress and maintain light elbow contact with each other. They marched straight and at oblique angles, and they practiced marching by file into line, transforming the marching column into a battlefront. It was dark when the sergeant finally marched them back into camp and dismissed them. Nathan and Christian realized that the boots they had been issued were not as comfortable as they first thought, and they winced as they sat on the ground in front of their shelter and took them off.

Billy was sitting on a log in front of his shelter wiping his musket down with a rag, by the light of a candle; he put in his bayonet socket and stuck it in the ground. "How'd it go, boys?"

Christian grunted. "My feet don't like me anymore."

"Wait 'til you march ten miles with full knapsack and musket."

"Perish the thought!" Christian stretched out on the ground and sighed. "I feel like I could sleep for a week."

"Don't get too comfortable just yet. I have a feeling you may be tapped for guard duty tonight. The first sergeant likes to sharpen up the fresh fish nice and quick."

As if on cue Corporal Purvill walked up and pointed to Nathan and Christian. "Butterfield and Taylor, you are on guard duty from three to five a.m. I will wake you when it's time." And with that, he walked off.

They looked at Billy as he calmly continued cleaning his musket. "We've all been through it. He'll put you with another private who's been here a while and can show you the ropes. You'll be fine. Probably want to turn in soon, though."

His advice made sense. They crawled into their shelter and under their blankets and did the best they could to get comfortable. Though the ground was hard and the sounds of men around them were distracting, the day caught up with them, and they soon succumbed to sleep. What seemed a second later, they were shaken awake and heard Purvill whisper, "Come on, boys, up and at 'em."

Groggily they stirred and fumbled around for their boots. Purvill said, "Bring your canteens and ponchos. It might rain."

As they finished gathering their gear and stood up, they were hit with cramps from their feet all the way up their legs. All they could do was gasp as quietly as they could and limp off behind Purvill, who kept whispering to them to keep up. They walked down the company street and toward the entrance of the camp, eventually stopping in front of a short, slight private standing by the fence. Purvill murmured to him and pointed to the two men, then approached them and said, "Private Benizzio will fill you in on your duties. Good night." He walked off and quickly faded into the darkness.

The two stood for a moment and then walked toward the private. Though it was difficult to tell in the darkness, he seemed to have a smirk on his face. Quietly, he said, "Judging from the way you two are walking, I'd say the cramps have got you pretty good." He spoke with an unmistakable Northeast accent. "I'm Paul Benizzio."

Nathan and Christian introduced themselves, and Christian continued. "So, what are we supposed to do?"

"We walk along this fence line to the corner, then we walk back and do it all over again. We're making sure the Army of Northern Virginia doesn't catch us by surprise." The two looked at him in surprise and he chuckled. "Actually, we're watching for wild animals prowling around, or men sneaking out of camp."

Nathan said, "What do you do if you see a wild animal?"

"I've only seen a few, and usually when I start walking toward them, they run off." "And what about men?"

"We're supposed to halt them, get their names, and bring them to the corporal on duty." He shrugged. "Depends on whether I know them or not."

Over the next two hours, they walked together back and forth along the fence line. Benizzio showed them how to stand guard, how to salute with a musket, and how to relieve a guard. He also showed them a very basic manual of arms including Order Arms, Support Arms, and Right Shoulder Shift Arms. He shared funny stories about his years growing up in Providence, Rhode Island. He talked about his winding journey from there to rural Pennsylvania and the pretty young wife and two cats who waited for him at home. He had strong opinions on the state of the war, of Lincoln and his cabinet, and especially of the Union military command. He did not think much of General McClellan and shook his head as he told of rumors he had heard that McClellan was soon to replace old Winfield Scott, hero of the War of 1812, as the general in chief of all Union forces. He occasionally asked questions of Nathan and Christian but gave them little time to answer before he jumped in with yet another story or opinion.

Though some might have been annoyed by the private's chattiness, Nathan and Christian were grateful for the company and the information he gave them as they walked in the darkness.

They were not too bothered by a gentle rain that started to fall, and soon after this, another corporal walked toward them with two sleepy privates in tow. He walked them through a proper report and relief, then dismissed the three to their shelters.

Days of routine blurred into weeks: awakened by fife and drum and shuffling into line at six a.m., meager breakfast, drill, lunch, various camp duties, more drill, supper, guard duty. The weather grew steadily colder. Rachael wrote often, keeping Nathan abreast of his father's condition, which improved with agonizing slowness. Joshua wrote occasionally and though he spoke with fondness of his work in the hospitals, Nathan also detected a tone of restlessness. He developed friendships with several men in the company and could not understand when Sergeant Jeremiah would warn the men not to become too close to each other.

He became intimately acquainted with his musket, the newly remodeled Springfield. Both Captain Shields and Jeremiah were almost fanatical about the men knowing how to disassemble, clean, and reassemble their weapons, to keep the barrels and powder dry, to unjam the muskets rapidly in the field, and to fire them accurately at a rate of three to four rounds a minute. The musket required nine movements to load and fire including the use of a rammer, which was difficult in a line of battle. It fired a .58-caliber lead slug, which spread on impact and, according to men who had already seen action, did horrible damage to the human body. Called the Minie ball after the French officer who invented it, the slug expanded with the heat from the exploding powder in the barrel until it fits neatly into grooves inside the musket barrel called rifling. Rifled barrels gave the slug a tight spin as it traveled down the barrel, which increased accuracy over the older round balls and unrifled barrels of the Napoleonic era from roughly fifty yards to almost two hundred yards.

The musket also came with a bayonet, which was surprisingly sharp at the tip, and in the course of bayonet drill, Nathan hoped never to be on the receiving end of such a charge. Billy and other veterans of previous engagements told Nathan and Christian that it was rarely a good idea to use the bayonet in close combat because it often became stuck in the body, and in the process of recovery, the attacker could just as easily be bayoneted himself. The veterans preferred using the butt of the stock as a club as it was much more efficient. Never comfortable with weapons before, Nathan learned all these things now and developed a healthy respect for his musket.

On a bitterly cold and windy morning in mid-November, Jeremiah called the company to fall in and quickly stepped aside as Captain Shields took command. In his clipped Yankee accent, he briefly informed the company that they would be participating in battalion drill, then marched them out of the camp and over a small ridge behind the camp, then along a road for several miles before turning off into a rather large plain. Other companies were also filing into the field from other directions, and in due course, each was halted while senior officers consulted in a small cluster. Finally, a tall, spare colonel stepped away from the group and began shouting orders in a clear and confident tone. Sergeants were sent scurrying by their captains to act as markers to dress their lines on the color guard, which formed in the middle of the battalion. When they were all formed according to specific company order, it was a spectacle to behold—nearly a thousand men at shoulder arms with fixed bayonets glinting in the sun.

What Nathan discovered was that battalion drill meant frequent periods of standing at attention while the senior officers conferred with each other, in between maneuvers of companies marching in line and then returning to the battlefront. It was during one of these long halts when Captain Shields mercifully ordered the company to rest so they could quickly drink from their canteens, that Nathan, standing in the rear rank, felt something hit the back of his head, and he noticed a pinecone roll to a stop at his feet. He looked behind him and immediately caught the familiar crooked grin of Matthew, standing in the front rank of the company directly behind Nathan's. Nathan was just about to say something when Captain Shields called the company to attention and so began another series of battalion maneuvers, this time through a stretch of pine barrens that ringed the plain, giving the battalion practice in moving efficiently around obstacles. Finally, the battalion was marched back to the plain and dressed in the colors, then unceremoniously dismissed. Captains again took command of their companies and most, including Captain Shields, ordered their men to fall out and rest a bit before they marched back to their camps.

Nathan and Christian seized the opportunity to find Matthew and his brothers and there followed a happy though short reunion. The brothers were in Company B and so far, seemed to have taken to military life. Stories and opinions were traded about officers and various personalities in each company, and Nathan realized how much he missed familiar faces from home. Too quickly, Sergeant Jeremiah was calling Company D to fall in, and Nathan and Christian hurriedly exchanged handshakes with the brothers before jogging back and finding a place in line. Jeremiah quickly sized and ordered the ranks, muskets were taken from standing stacks the men had formed in front of the company, and Captain Shields marched the men away to a brisk drumbeat.

Arriving back at camp in the early afternoon, the company was fed lunch, guard details were set, and the rest of the men were given some rare time to rest. Most went directly to sleep, exhausted from the morning of standing and marching. Nathan and Christian spent time writing letters home, energized by the unexpected meeting with their friends.

The company settled into a dull routine over the next several weeks—company drill, skirmish drill, battalion drill, guard duty, water detail, and wood detail. The weather grew colder, and soon snow was on the ground, stirring the men to become inventive in creating warm shelter for themselves. Some efforts were fairly successful; others ended in near disaster as men discovered that canvas was quite flammable. The men were disappointed to learn that there would be no furloughs home for Christmas, but this was tempered by their growing faith in the little dynamo that was their general-in-chief. He worked with seemingly boundless energy to equip and train the Union forces to such a degree that they would be well-nigh invincible.

Though Lincoln and his cabinet began to grow restless at the slow pace of retooling the fighting forces of the North, the men in the ranks maintained that Little Mac knew what he was about, and they pledged to follow him to Richmond and beyond.

***

My dearest Nathan,

It is hard to believe that you and Christian have already been gone for several months. I miss you both terribly (Christian more, as I hope you understand). Christmas was not the same without your calm and smiling face at the table. I could tell that Father missed you as well, though he attempted to put on a brave front. I hope that the socks I sent you both (made by the loving hands of women from the church) will be of good use and comfort to you.

We are doing well here in general. Little Micah continues to grow rapidly and amazes me almost every day in his development. I long for the time when his papa and his Uncle Joshua can hold him again. My family in Pittsburgh has been of immense help in caring for him, such that I have been able to continue pursuing my writing, though obviously not with the same fervor as I had before my precious little one was born.

We see Joshua fairly often in between his various hospital endeavors. There seems a restlessness in him these days, Nathan. He reads much of war news and sees more of his colleagues volunteering in state regiments, and my heart grows cold at the thought of it. Will we have all of our young men become a part of this foolish conflict, which will only bring loss and sorrow to so many?

Father is quiet these days. I am afraid that he will not progress much more in his daily functioning. He contents himself in reading the Bible and praying, though often he drifts into sleep in the process.

I must close now. My little man is waking from his nap and calls for me. Nathan, please take good care of yourself. I love you more than you know. Keep a watchful eye on Christian.

Please do not tell him this, but I find it somewhat difficult to believe that he could adapt to a soldier's life. I am so dreadfully afraid that he will hurt himself in some way before he ever experiences battle. I know that I should trust in God to keep you both safe, but I cannot help yearning for your safety. God bless you, dear

Nathan until we meet again.

With great affection, Rachael

***

The days continued to blur one into another. The only interesting events were seeing new recruits join the company and the slow trickle of news regarding future movements of the army. It seemed almost every man had a theory based on a smattering of facts, and theories were trotted out and evaluated during guard duty, around evening fires, and in shelters during the small hours of the night. Most, including Christian, believed that the army would be marching any day toward Richmond. The officers were not much help, busy as they were with reports to their unit commanders and following strict orders to quell any fantastical rumors. Nathan did not have a strong opinion, but he had learned to pay attention to the veterans in the company. These men quietly shook their heads whenever others began to conjecture. They seemed to feel an invisible pulse, and their instincts told them that McClellan would move very slowly and carefully. Billy was of this mind, and he told Nathan and Christian more than once, "When you start seeing officers scurrying around like ants with their nest kicked over, something important is about to happen."

One rumor actually did materialize. Nathan had heard men talking at supper one evening that McClellan himself was to review their regiment sometime in the coming days. Nathan did not believe it until the morning of the next battalion drill when he noticed that the officers seemed unusually nervous and were more particular about the men's appearance. Muskets and brass were to be rigorously polished, leathers blackened, uniforms repaired, and as clean as possible. Upon marching into the familiar field, Nathan noticed a large entourage of officers on horseback, positioned on a small rise. The dress of the battalion seemed particularly crisp that morning, sternly guided by the senior regimental officers. As the battalion stood at attention, the group on the rise moved slowly down, and now Nathan could see a smallish figure in the lead astride a magnificent horse, his officer's kepi set jauntily on his head. Slowly the group wound its way through the lines of companies. When they passed by Company D, though the men had been given strict orders by Captain Shields to keep eyes front, Nathan snuck a quick glance at this man who commanded legions. He had a somewhat handsome face and a luxurious mustache, and his posture was ramrod straight. Other than that, Nathan thought him quite ordinary. The group rode slowly back to the rise, McClellan had a brief conversation with the regimental colonel, and then McClellan and his group rode off. Drill seemed lighter and shorter that day, and Nathan wondered if this was the way the colonel expressed his pleasure with the regiment's review.

For a few days the men of Company D, mostly the new recruits, talked excitedly about the visit from Little Mac, but this soon died down and routine took over. It was not long, however, before the routine took a marked turn. Billy was one of the first to notice the changes. Captain Shields had more meetings with officers in his tent. Drill was increased, particularly for skirmish.

Guards were doubled. Delivery of supplies greatly increased such that the quartermaster had to erect several more tents to accommodate the material. Finally, one gloomy morning in early March, Captain Shields had the company assembled and announced in his curt manner that the regiment was to begin marching south the next morning. The company was to spend most of the day striking the camp in preparation. Sergeants were given instructions to create details of various kinds, the company was dismissed, and the work began. Nathan and Christian were bone-tired at the end of the day and sat quietly on log stumps by a small fire in front of their tent. Billy ambled by and pulled up a log, and the three men sat in silence for a few minutes. Finally Christian spoke.

"Billy, why do you think we're moving now?"

"I think Washington has been leaning on McClellan hard to get this army going, and he's finally giving in to the pressure." Nathan stirred the fire.

"Why haven't we moved until now?"

"McClellan is very cautious. Maybe too cautious. I think he's got it in his head that everything has to be perfect before he sets things in motion. And I think he believes there's a huge Rebel force out there somewhere just waiting to swoop down on us."

"Is there?"

Billy gave a low chuckle. "Hell if I know. But we're not accomplishing anything by just sitting in a field in Pennsylvania."

After a few more minutes of small talk, the men succumbed to the rigors of the day and turned in, knowing that they would be wakened early to start the march south.

The next several days were some of the most physically punishing of Nathan's life. He had tried to pack light, but even so, his knapsack was full and the straps bit into his shoulders. His musket was an annoyance no matter what position he tried. It rained on and off, and the thousands of tramping boots, horse hooves, wagon, and caisson wheels churned the roads into a quagmire.

Camps were dreary affairs, and sleep was only made possible by sheer exhaustion, which finally overcame the pain of cramping muscles. The initial fascination of observing a huge army on the move quickly shifted to a focus on personal misery. Gradually, however, Nathan began to adjust to the rigors of marching and began to join conversations with men who marched beside him.

The army moved slowly, as Billy's theorizing of McClellan had predicted. McClellan had contracted with Allan Pinkerton's national detective agency to gather information on the Confederate army. Pinkerton, who had made a name for himself by foiling an alleged assassination plot against President Lincoln earlier in the year, had the unfortunate habit of significantly overestimating enemy troop numbers. This fed into McClellan's already cautious nature such that the Army of the Potomac at times marched only several miles in a day, though at least in theory, it was capable of much more.

McClellan's plan was to march the army down to the Chesapeake Bay and embark on ships that would carry the fighting force to Fort Monroe, then to march up the peninsula between the York and James Rivers on its way to the Confederate capitol at Richmond, Virginia. The plan had the potential for boldness and speed on paper, but McClellan's overabundance of caution neutralized these advantages. As the army approached the bay, McClellan halted the army yet again, having heard that the Confederates had attacked part of the Union fleet in Hampton Roads near the bay with an unusual vessel known as an ironclad. Though the Union eventually chased off the intruder with its own ironclad after a two-day duel, two Union ships and hundreds of lives were lost in the battle, and more time was lost for the Army of the Potomac, allowing for the Confederate army to gather its strength and mount a defense.

Eventually, the Union troops got moving again, made their way down the Chesapeake and disembarked at Fort Monroe, and began their march up the peninsula. For all of McClellan's hesitation, the landing and staging of a staggering number of men and materiel were handled with surprising efficiency. In fairly short order, regiments and wagons and artillery batteries were sorted out and sent marching off from the fort to the accompaniment of fife and drum. The men of Pennsylvania took their place in the gigantic column and set their faces northeast.

That evening the army was halted after a fairly brisk march, and McClellan ordered the cavalry to move ahead and reconnoiter the territory. After a brief consultation with a major from the regiment, Captain Shields led Company D to a small grove of trees. The company mess was organized, water and wood details were sent out, and pickets were set around the perimeter of the camp. Supper was a quiet affair and many men turned in early, tired from the day. They were awakened early the next morning, and the army moved off, beginning a very slow march up toward Richmond.

The pattern of short marches and frequent halts continued for the next two weeks without incident, until the army neared Yorktown. One afternoon on the march, word began to pass down the column that the Confederates were dug in up ahead and putting up a fight. It was not long before the faint sound of musket and cannon fire reached the men in the ranks, and very quickly conversation ceased. Nathan saw a major canter down the side of the column and rein in beside Captain Shields. He leaned over and said something briefly to the captain, then rode on down the column to the next regiment. Captain Shields halted the company and called the sergeants to him. Nathan looked a few ranks ahead and saw Billy, standing very still and quiet. After a few minutes the sergeants returned to their places in the ranks and soon after that the column started forward again, but this time only a short distance until they came to an open expanse dotted with trees. Regiments were grouped into their brigades and ordered to rest.

Captain Shields kept Company D at attention and addressed them. The sounds of battle were louder now, but his voice carried and every man was listening closely. "As you can hear, we are in contact with the enemy. We don't yet know their strength or their exact position, so our company has been ordered up with some others for skirmishers on the right flank of the army. Sergeants will check cartridge boxes and cap pouches to make sure each man is well-supplied. Drink plenty of water while they are doing that, and then we will move out with the other companies. Remember your training. Listen to your sergeants and corporals. Keep your mouths shut and your eyes open and stay together."

For the next few minutes, all that could be heard above the battle sounds was the opening and closing of boxes and pouches, the clinking of canteens, and the occasional comment from one of the sergeants. Nathan could feel his heart beating faster and his hands sweating. Captain Shields called the company to attention and ordered muskets loaded and bayonets fixed, and marched them into a column of other companies, which headed off to the right, away from the main body of the army. After several hundred yards the column was ordered to march at left oblique, and then each company was split off and formed into two lines of skirmishers, with approximately ten feet between each man and twenty feet between the lines.

Nathan looked to his right and noticed Christian several men down, his eyes wide and serious. Suddenly he heard a sound like a large bumblebee close to his head. As the lines stepped off, he heard several more of these sounds, and suddenly one of the men on his left cried out, dropped his musket, and clutched his leg. Now Nathan saw clods of dirt and grass kicked into the air in front of the first line of skirmishers. Captain Shields' voice rang out sharp and clear, "Fire at will!"

Men on either side stopped, kneeled, and fired, then quickly began to reload. Nathan looked ahead and could see grey smoke rising through a line of trees, shadowy figures standing, and the occasional flash of sun on musket barrels. A man in front of him spun and fell on his back, and as Nathan walked by him, he saw a bloody socket where the man's left eye had been.

The noise of muskets grew louder. Almost in a trance, Nathan kneeled, aimed his musket at the shadows in the trees, fired, and began to reload. More men in front and beside him screamed in pain or fell down. The sergeant behind him bellowed, "Find cover where you can!"

Nathan fumbled in his cartridge box and finally grabbed a cartridge, put the tail between his teeth, and ripped. Much of the gunpowder spilled into his mouth and he gagged and spit. He managed to pour the rest down the musket barrel and push the ball down with his thumb. The lines were slowly moving ahead of him now, and he began to panic. He drew his ramrod and dropped it in the tall grass. Frantically he looked for it, found it, and completed loading. Just as he brought the musket up to his shoulder something heavy fell on him and knocked him flat to the ground. His breath was driven out of him, and the hammer mechanism of his musket jabbed into his ribs. Suddenly, the weight lifted, and Nathan rolled over to see a sergeant holding a man by the collar of his sack coat. He threw the man to the side and shouted to Nathan, "You OK, soldier?"

Nathan nodded, still catching his breath. The sergeant offered him a hand and pulled him to his feet. "Helluva scrap we're in. Now move up to your place in the line."

Nathan nodded again and jogged forward. He quickly caught up to the line and noticed that it seemed shorter. Another sergeant grabbed him by the shoulder and shoved him into a gap. They were much closer to the trees now, and the musket fire was almost deafening. Christian was nowhere in sight. Suddenly, there was a deep concussive boom and a huge spray of dirt, followed closely by another boom. Three men in the front line were thrown into the air like rag dolls and landed awkwardly. Captain Shields appeared on the left with sword drawn, shouting, "On the ground, men, on the ground!"

Quickly men threw themselves down and hugged the earth as shells began to whistle and burst around them. Captain Shields grabbed a lieutenant and yelled a message, and the lieutenant ran toward the rear. Nathan watched as the lieutenant flagged down a major on horseback and pointed toward the tree line, shouting a message. The major nodded and wheeled his horse and dug his spurs in, and at that moment a shell exploded under the horse. The major's right arm came off at the shoulder and he was thrown up into a tree. The horse was blown nearly in half, its entrails scattered across the ground. The lieutenant, thrown off his feet by the blast, rose shakily and stood for a moment before jogging toward the rear.

There was a brief lull in the firing, and Nathan began to hear shouts and whoops from the trees in front. Captain Shields quickly called for an orderly retreat, and the lines began to creep backward, firing as they went. Several more men fell as they retreated across the field, others rising and limping back with the company as best they could. After a few hundred yards, Captain Shields called the company to attention and marched them by files to the right. As Nathan looked to his right, he could see long and tightly packed lines of men in blue marching toward them with flags flying. He knew that he should be happy to see reinforcements coming up, but he was numb. His ears were ringing, and there was a pain in his ribs.

The captain marched the company to a small copse of trees and ordered them to rest and drink water. The sounds of battle swelled again as the main body began to push through the tree line. This time there was an added sound, that of men screaming and moaning in pain. It was an unnerving sound, but Nathan was too stunned to raise his hands to his ears. He sat slumped on the ground with his back against a tree, staring at nothing. After several moments he realized that someone was talking to him, and he slowly raised his head. Christian sat down beside him and put a hand on his shoulder. His face was smeared with black powder and dirt, and his forage cap was gone. He smiled, but the smile did not touch his eyes. "Good God, Nathan. I don't know what to say."

For a few moments, Nathan did not move or speak. Then, very slowly, he raised a hand and put it on Christian's hand. They stayed that way for a long time as the sounds of battle rose and fell around them. Eventually, the company was called to attention, and they moved woodenly into line. They were marched back the way they had come and encamped near a swamp.

The line at the mess tent was shorter that evening. Nathan and Christian got their food and walked back to their tent and sat. Nathan stared at the food in his pan but did not touch it. Billy came by and sat; a cigar clamped between his teeth. He had a cloth bandage around his neck. He breathed deeply and looked at the two men in front of him. "Well, now you've seen the elephant."

Christian stirred. "What did you say?"

"Seeing the elephant. You've heard about battle and trained for it, now you've been in it." Hearing no reply, Billy continued. "Seems we bumped into the main Rebel body sooner than expected. We got pulled back just in time to miss the main ball." He shook his head. "Whoever said Reb artillery is ineffective is a damned idiot. They kicked our asses but good today."

Nathan looked up for the first time and saw the bandage. "You okay, Billy?"

"Yeah, I'm fine. Just got nicked by some shrapnel as we were falling back. I've had worse."

They talked softly for a while longer and then, by unspoken agreement, turned in. Nathan lay awake in the darkness, listening to the peepers in the swamp and other night sounds. The taste of gunpowder was still in his mouth, and his ribs ached. Worse than that were the sights and sounds from the day that paraded through his mind. He finally fell into an exhausted sleep and dreamed of human arms catapulting through a forest.

The next several weeks were a grueling stretch of marching, digging in, skirmishes, and pitched battles. McClellan continued to envision untold Confederate legions in front of him and crept forward ever so cautiously, though in actuality he fielded more than four times the number of enemy troops he faced. His counterpart, Joseph Johnston, also cautious but a solid tactician continued to give ground slowly up the peninsula in such a way that he was able to feed McClellan's paranoia. Secretary of War Edwin Stanton paced in his office, yelled at his secretaries, and threw papers; Lincoln sent telegrams with increasing urgency and sarcastic bite, but still, McClellan crawled.

The men in the field by and large were still with their commander, but some were becoming jaundiced at the slow pace. Rumors circulated that McClellan and his staff had ridden close enough to Richmond to hear church bells and that the capitol city was guarded only by a ragtag group of old men and boys. But when George B. rode through the camps on his magnificent horse, resplendent in a spotless uniform, most soldiers still waved their caps and cheered. He was their man for now, and they believed he would lead them to Richmond and glory.

Nathan was becoming a different man. On the outside, he was calm and focused, sharp and vigorous in drill, and efficient in battle. He was treated with growing respect by men in the company. Sergeant Jeremiah noticed and suggested he consider corporal stripes, but Nathan respectfully declined.

On the inside he was hardening, diminishing. It was as though the losses earlier in his life had waited quietly like cancerous cells, and now the horrors of battle had wakened them, and they were eating away his soul. He felt no joy. He did what was in front of him to do with a cold energy, and then he shut down at night. Christian noticed this and asked him if he was all right and received only shallow assurances and a grim smile. Not knowing what else to do, Christian wrote a concerned letter to Rachael. Nathan in turn received a letter from her soon after.

***

My dearest Nathan,

Though normally I would begin my letter with pleasantries about how the family and I doing (briefly, all are generally well though Micah seems susceptible to colds), I am dispensing with the usual structure because of a letter I recently received from Christian. Nathan, he is quite concerned about you. If you feel the need to tell him that I have told you about the letter he sent me, I understand. At any rate, he tells me that you are not yourself, that you are more brooding and intense than usual, and that there is a darkness about you. My dear brother, I cannot hope to ever understand the horrors you have experienced in battle. I do not know how any man's mind can deal with such events. I have learned a bit as I have started volunteering in the hospital—hearing the soldiers talk about their experiences, seeing their physical wounds, and sensing their emotional ones.

I pray every day that you and Christian will return safely to us one day very soon, body and soul. Please know that many people are praying for your protection. Believe that good is being done even amid great suffering and loss. Understand that God is sovereign, that His ways are higher than our ways and that He is working out His plans even when we do not understand what He is doing. Remember that you have a family who loves you deeply. Do not give in to darkness and despair, even when you are surrounded by it. Be sustained by the thought that I am waiting to embrace you and tell you that all will be well. Come back to us, Nathan.

With more love than you can know, Rachael

***

The night that Nathan received the letter he sat on the ground outside his shelter and stared off into the darkness. He did not register the murmur of conversations, the occasional laughter, or the cheerful sounds of a far-off banjo. He thought only about God—the awesome and mysterious Watchmaker of the universe, looking down dispassionately on His creation and choosing not to intervene while men killed and maimed each other by the thousands. The ideas of God being sovereign and working out some grand cosmic plan ate at his mind like acid. He knew that Rachael believed the words she had written to him with all her heart, but though he loved her, he thought her a fool. He would believe what he could see, and nothing more.

His bitterness only grew as the army pushed its way up the peninsula. The Union ranks were being thinned, and new recruits were being thrown into the gaps only to be slaughtered within days. The Confederate commander Johnston was wounded and replaced by Robert E. Lee, who had his troops dig in so often that they called him the King of Spades. But his defensive methods worked and combined with McClellan's extreme caution to finally halt the Union juggernaut short of its objective. Then Lee's true genius was revealed as he shifted to the offensive, throwing a series of assaults at the hesitant enemy that would become known as the Seven Days. The Union army was pushed relentlessly back down the peninsula in the face of the onslaught, with McClellan seemingly powerless to stem the tide.

For Nathan and the men of his company, indeed for every Union soldier on the peninsula, it was a waking nightmare. They fought in the heat and the rain, through thickets and swamps and uneven terrain, and inexorably backward. The smell of the dead lying on the open ground was ghastly. Worse still was the sight of feral pigs digging up and eating bodies that had been hastily buried. The final blow came when McClellan decided to turn and attack the Confederate lines on a rise of ground known as Malvern Hill. Lee was more than ready and easily repulsed the Union attack, inflicting heavy losses. This effectively signaled the end of the peninsula campaign and humiliated the Army of the Potomac.

In the evening after the battle, Luke, Nathan's former neighbor, shuffled into Company D's camp and found Nathan and Christian. The haunted look in his eyes told the story immediately, but the two men waited while he sat and breathed deeply, tears making trails through the dirt on his face. Finally, he told them that his brother Matthew had been killed on one of the final assaults up the hill and that Mark was in a hospital tent and might lose a leg. Nathan and Christian immediately offered to go with him to visit Mark, and after a few shuddering breaths, he nodded, and they got up and walked together. Nathan found a sergeant and received permission for the two men to see their friend.

They smelled the hospital tent before they saw it. The sickly-sweet smell of blood mixed with sweat and urine and laudanum to create an odor that made them gag. Gradually they heard the screams and moans and delirious babbling of the wounded, and the whine of bone saws. As they approached the tent, they saw a surgeon with a blood-soaked apron slumped tiredly on a bench, and beside him a pile of arms and legs taller than his head. The light from oil lamps inside the tent cast ghostly moving shadows on the canvas walls. The men removed their caps, took a deep breath, and entered.

Grim desperation met their eyes. Immediately to their left a man lay on a table, shouting and struggling mightily under the grip of three orderlies while a doctor sawed on one leg above the knee. A man sat propped against a tent pole holding his own intestines in with his bare hands. Nurses bent over cots and whispered gently to men who were little more than boys, crying out for their mothers. In one corner a young musician knelt beside his drum and sobbed as the man on the cot in front of him, clearly a member of his family, talked to him in a low and earnest voice.

The three men walked quietly down the middle of the tent until Luke recognized his brother and stopped. Mark had his head propped up by a pillow, his eyes closed. The left side of his face was bloody, and his ear was gone. His left leg below the knee was a gory mess. Luke looked stricken. He called a nearby nurse to clean his brother up. When she did not answer he swore and yelled at her. She turned slowly and glowered at him. Then she picked up a bucket with water and a rag and marched up to him and shoved the bucket into his chest. In a thick Irish brogue, she growled, "Here, ya' foul-mouthed hooligan. Clean him up yerself. I'm attendin' ta' three men who will soon be passin' over." And with that, she turned on her heel and walked over to another cot.

The three men exchanged brief glances. Then Luke walked to his brother's cot and set the bucket down. He dipped the rag in the water and wrung it out, then began to gently dab at his brother's face. Mark stirred and opened his eyes. Some moments passed before he focused on Luke's face. His eyes flickered and a tiny smile passed across his lips. He started to speak, cleared his throat, and tried again. "Water?"

Christian handed his canteen to Luke, who put it to Mark's mouth for a small drink. Mark swallowed and sighed. "Well, brother, how do I look?"

Luke gave a small shake of his head. "Like death warmed over, which is an improvement." "You heard about Matthew?"

"Yes," was all Luke could manage, his chin quivering and his eyes filling with tears. "What will mother say?"

"She will be crushed."

"Yes, she will." Mark shifted his weight and grimaced, then looked up at Luke. "And what of my leg? I know it's bad, but ..."

Luke looked desperately at Nathan and Christian, and all they could do was return his gaze. He looked back helplessly at his brother. "Well, I don't know. I haven't talked to a surgeon, so—"

Mark grabbed his arm suddenly, fear in his eyes. "Don't let them cut it off! Surely there's something they can do to save it!"

Luke closed his eyes. "Please, brother!"

A nurse came over with a look of concern. "Is there anything I can do to help?" Luke turned to her. "My brother's leg. Has it been looked at by a surgeon yet?" "I'm not sure. He has been so busy since— "

"He needs to know!"

She sighed and motioned for Luke to wait. She walked over to the surgeon, who had finished an amputation and was overseeing an orderly bandaging the wound. The nurse put a hand on the surgeon's shoulder and whispered to him, pointing in Mark's direction. The surgeon walked over and looked quickly at Mark's leg. His jaw muscles tightened momentarily, then he looked at Mark and Luke in turn. "I'm sorry, but the leg will have to come off." He wiped his hands on his apron and walked away.

The nurse went to Mark and put a hand on his shoulder. "It will be all right, son."

"Get your hand off me!" he shouted. He reached out for Luke. "Don't let them do this!" Luke stood like a statue.

"Luke!"

Nathan stepped forward and gripped both of Mark's shoulders. "Listen to me! Your leg is a mess. If they don't take it off, you will die of disease, and by God, you do not want that. Now get hold of yourself!"

He held Mark's gaze fiercely until he saw the fear begin to recede. He gently released his hold and stepped back. Mark swallowed twice and closed his eyes for a few moments. When he opened them again, he was calm. He looked at Luke, who had still not moved.

"Visit me again soon, brother." He reached out a hand.

Luke shuffled forward and took the hand in both of his and nodded. Christian put a hand gently on Luke's shoulder and said, "Well, I think we'd best be going." To Mark, he said, "Rest easy, my friend. We'll see you before too long." He paused, then said quietly, "And we will get a letter to your mother about you and Matthew."

Mark looked up with lifeless eyes and mumbled, "No. I will take care of that." With that, he slowly turned his head away.

The three walked out of the tent without a word. Nathan and Christian took their leave of Luke at the Company B encampment. They heard him say goodbye, but his mouth did not seem to move. They walked silently back in the dark to their own camp, checked in with a sergeant, and turned into their shelter.

Nathan lay awake for a long time. Gradually, the sounds of the camp died down until all he could hear were men sleeping and the crackle of a fire. After what seemed like hours, he sighed and crawled out of the shelter. He walked to a small brushy area and relieved himself, exchanging a few words with the pickets before walking back. Just before he reached his shelter, he looked to his left and saw the chaplain sitting at a fire. He changed course and approached.

"Can I join you, sir?"

The old man smiled and motioned to a nearby log. "Make yourself to home, Private. I was just talking with the Lord about today's events."

Nathan sat and looked into the fire for several minutes before speaking. "What is it like for you, talking to God?"

"Like speaking with an old and dear friend." Ericcson stopped and looked at Nathan. "I imagine you're wondering how I know He is listening."

Nathan nodded.

"Well, young man, I choose to believe what the Good Word says about that. It comes down to faith that God means what He says."

"What about when you ask Him for something and it doesn't happen?"

The chaplain looked at Nathan for a long moment. "You mean like good people continuing to die?"

Nathan stood up. "I just visited a friend in the hospital tonight. I grew up with him and his family. His brother was killed in the fight today. His father and another brother died years ago. My friend will lose a leg. That is too much loss for one family."

"Yes, it is."

Nathan put a fresh log on the fire and watched the sparks dance upward into the darkness. "Is that all you have to say?"

"What do you want me to say? That these events are unfair? That the family did not deserve them? That God doesn't care?" The chaplain's tone had taken on a harder edge.

Nathan was taken aback at the response. "Well, yes."

"Do you think I have the answers to these questions?"

"I thought that maybe you could—"

"Well, I don't." The chaplain softened. "Most of the time, I don't know why God does what He does, and believe me, I have spent many years trying to understand. So where does that leave us?"

Nathan was silent, listening intently.

Ericcson leaned forward, his eyes shining in the firelight. "I choose to believe that God wants us to spend our lives getting to know as much of Him as we possibly can, and to trust Him with those things we do not understand." He looked up to the night sky. "I believe that the God who made the stars and the vast heavens knows what He is doing." He pointed to Nathan and then himself. "I believe that He knows every part of our being, every thought and emotion we have. He knows we are capable of great good and yet our hearts draw us toward evil. He knows that we cannot change our hearts on our own and because of that, we cannot be near Him." He leaned farther forward and spoke very softly. "And yet, He loved us enough to make a way for us to be forever changed, through the sacrifice of his Son, so that we can be with God all the time." The chaplain leaned back with a blissful smile on his face. "He is always, always working for our good, through all circumstances."

Nathan shook his head. "I still cannot believe that suffering is for our good. Especially for those who don't deserve it."

"How do you know that? Do you know more than God?" The chaplain smiled wryly. "My boy, men much smarter than you or I have been wrestling with these things for thousands of years, and there is no consensus yet. To my mind, it comes down to believing that either God is sovereign and loving, or He is not." He rose and stretched. "I think I am finally beginning to feel tired." He walked around the fire and stopped briefly to squeeze Nathan's shoulder. "I will be praying that God will grant both of us greater understanding in the days to come. Good night, Private Butterfield." He walked off into the darkness, leaving Nathan with his thoughts.

Nathan received a letter two days later as the company was starting to break camp. It was from Joshua, and it caused Nathan's heart to sink. Joshua had met some soldiers as he made rounds in the hospitals in Pittsburgh, and after hearing their honest and sobering accounts of the fighting, he had felt the call to join the ranks. He had passed his position to a colleague, said goodbye to their father and Rachael, enlisted, and given permission to join Company B at the earliest opportunity.

It was a miserable Army of the Potomac that sat on the James Peninsula that summer. McClellan moved his troops a short distance and then had them dig in, while he bandied back and forth with the White House. Eventually, Lincoln lost his patience and began to transfer much of McClellan's command to John Pope and his Army of Virginia. Pope was a former railroad surveyor with command experience in the Mexican War and most recently in the western theatre, where he had achieved some success. He had led troops near the Shiloh battlefield in Tennessee just the past April, though he missed most of the horrendous two-day struggle and in some ways was still an unknown quantity. McClellan fumed and argued at length, but he had taxed the good graces of the War Department and the President past the breaking point.

If the sensibilities of the Little Napoleon had been offended, things were much worse for the men in the ranks. They had time to rest and recover, but not necessarily in comfort. Heavy rains turned encampments into cesspools where disease ran rampant and finished off many of the wounded. The steaming heat of Virginia made daily camp life nearly unbearable and even felled some through heat stroke. Worse than these was the pall of defeat that lay heavy on them. They sensed that victory had been within their grasp, but their commander had let them down. Discontent led to grumbling and fighting and challenging authority, and nervous officers implemented harsh discipline in response. Nathan's regiment was witness to several whippings for minor infractions and the deaths of several soldiers by firing squad due to attempts to desert. The effect of this approach was to restore at best a fragile order.

One muggy evening Nathan and several others sat around a fire. That day the regiment had been called to assembly for yet another punishment, this time a soldier being drummed out of the ranks for raping a civilian woman, and the mood in the camp was somber. Nathan watched Billy clean his musket yet again. Benizzio was idly whittling a stick, holding his knife in a new way since losing three fingers in the recent campaign. A newer private was reading a newspaper aloud, recounting yet another Union defeat in the Shenandoah Valley at the hands of the eccentric and brilliant Stonewall Jackson. Christian had left earlier, saying he was off to see if the sutlers had anything decent to buy. These merchants often followed the army and set up their tents and wares with surprising speed, selling everything from photographic likenesses to homemade pies, things not provided by the quartermaster corps. Nathan was beginning to wonder what had become of Christian when he heard a voice behind him.

"Look what I found."

Nathan turned and there, standing by Christian, was his brother. Joshua wore a new uniform that looked somewhat small for him. He had the beginnings of a beard, and his skin was pale, but otherwise, it was the Joshua he remembered. Nathan stood slowly and walked to him.

Joshua flashed a crooked grin and held out his arms, and they embraced warmly. After a moment Nathan stepped back and looked Joshua in the eyes. "It is good to see you, brother. You look terrible."

Joshua burst out laughing. "I could say the same about you."

Nathan quickly gave introductions, and the other men made room for Joshua to sit by the fire. After a deep breath and a swallow of whiskey offered by Billy from a hip flask, Joshua clapped Nathan on the shoulder and said, "So, soldier brother. Tell me about the life."

For the next hour and more Nathan and the others regaled Joshua with tales of daily camp, the rigors of marching, and tips the veterans had learned about such things as making a fire and cooking quickly, getting through inspections, and putting up with difficult officers. When Joshua asked for more specific details of battles, the men grew quieter and offered little. He shared with them what newspapers reported of the war in the field and in the capital, and was surprised at the difference between printed stories and actual experience. Gradually, the other men grew tired and went off to their shelters, but the two brothers and Christian remained. Nathan put a few more logs on the fire and sat down next to Joshua.

"Well, how are things at home?"

Joshua sighed. "The hospitals are overflowing with the sick and wounded from the battlefields. We are trying to staff the best we can, but we've lost many orderlies to the ranks. Thank God for Clara Barton, who is training up more nurses for us."

"We have musicians do orderly work around here much of the time," Christian said quietly. "It is a sobering thing to watch a ten-year-old boy gather the remains of a man into a wheelbarrow with a shovel after that man has been hit with canister fire from close range."

"I cannot begin to imagine." Joshua was quiet for a minute before speaking again. "Micah is growing like a weed. Rachael told me to send her love to both of you, but ..."

Nathan looked up. "But what?"

Joshua smiled shyly. "I'm not going to kiss you both as she asked me to."

"Well, that's a relief," Nathan said with a chuckle. "How is Father?"

"Up and down. Some days, he seems to be winding down to the end; other days he is stubborn and fiery as ever. Still can't talk, but he's done a bit of writing."

"On what subject?" Christian asked.

"Church history, I think. An itinerant pastor has been called in to preach, but the board wants Father to feel useful, bless them."

"Yes," Nathan nodded. "They have been good to our family."

Joshua stretched. "And what of the company chaplain? What is he like, then?"

"Old Swede. The men make fun of his accent and his rambling sermons when he's not around."

"Does he make any sense? Is he true to the Word?"

"He . . . " Nathan paused. "He is sharper than most give him credit for."

"Hmm. I would like to talk with this man soon. See what he thinks of the Reformers."

They talked a while longer until tiredness overcame them, and they turned into their shelters. Joshua's assigned shelter mate was already asleep and sounded like a sawmill in full swing. Joshua gingerly took off his brogans and settled onto his straw bedding the best he could, wondering what he had gotten himself into.

He was rudely awakened just after daybreak by the shelter mate's pet rooster, crowing for all it was worth. Joshua had not seen it the night before because it had the habit of flying up into a nearby tree to sleep. His shelter mate, a burly and foul-mouthed farmer named Maxwell, snorted and yelled, "Enough, Bragg!" The rooster called twice more and then fell silent, apparently satisfied with its work. It was impossible to sleep after that, as the camp began to stir and rouse itself for the day.

Among other things, Joshua learned from his rough new companion at breakfast that morning was the origin of the rooster's name. "General Braxton Bragg, Rebel general out west. One crotchety old son of a bitch from what I'm told. I found this rooster near an abandoned farmhouse on the way down the Peninsula just screeching to beat all hell, and the name just came to me." With that Maxwell threw his head back and gave a raspy laugh, then promptly packed a plug of tobacco into his bottom lip and stomped off to relieve himself.

Joshua proved himself to be a quick study of the soldier's life over the next several weeks, which was good because finally, the army began to move. News had been given to Pope's staff by scouts in the area that Lee was pushing north toward Washington with his Army of Northern Virginia. The new commander of the Army of Virginia, eager to make points with the War Department, responded quickly to their urgent telegraphs and followed the grey fox, determined to cut him off and destroy the threat. Joshua dashed off a letter to Ezra one evening after a long and dusty march, apprising the old man of the military situation and providing colorful commentary on the details of campaigning.

Christian also wrote a letter, to Rachael, as he had consistently since joining the company. He wanted to reassure her the best he could that he was well, so he was careful to share only general comments about the battles he had faced. Rachael in turn was equally faithful in returning his letters. She spoke glowingly of their son's health and development. She also shared excerpts from her writings. She continued with her women's writing group and found what she thought was a worthy topic for her craft. She had spent some time volunteering in a hospital in Pittsburgh and met some interesting men as they convalesced. Their personal stories inspired her to write a series of biographical articles on these soldiers, "to put more of a face to this war" as she stated in her most recent letter. One article, for example, focused on a soldier from Minnesota who had quit his uncle's lumber mill in Stillwater and joined the First Minnesota Volunteer Infantry Regiment out of Fort Snelling in St. Paul. He was an interesting character in his own right, and the unit from the young prairie state had already served with distinction in the Army of the Potomac's Second Corps. Rachael hoped that *Harper's Weekly* might at some point choose to print this and her other articles, but she was not holding her breath.

If Joshua thought he was going to see battle soon, he was mistaken. As the opposing armies closed on the old Manassas battleground from the previous year, the regiment was detached to help guard wagon trains and an artillery park. The men found rotted and rusty debris scattered near their encampment, as well as some human remains. One former actor from Company C found a skull and gave a stirring rendition of Hamlet's speech, winning hoots and whistles from an audience largely new to Shakespeare.

Over the next two days, they heard the roar of battle and received updates from artillery crews as they were relieved or came back for supplies. On the march north, Billy had requested to be transferred to an artillery unit and had joined a battery only days ago. On the afternoon of the first day, Nathan found him loading a caisson with ordnance and asked him how the battle was going. He gently placed another shell in the wagon and turned to Nathan with a grim look.

"Far as I can tell, it's chaos. I think we're facing Jackson's corps, and he isn't giving any ground." He took a quick drink from his canteen and excused himself with a wave of his massive hand. Nathan wished him well and watched as the team pulled out of the park at a gallop.

As evening fell on the second day, the sounds of battle began to quiet, and stragglers shared details in bits and pieces. Pope had concentrated too much on attacking Jackson's troops and had been unaware until too late that Longstreet had pushed through a gap in the Union lines and joined with Jackson. Longstreet's counterattack crushed the Union left flank and sent Pope's army reeling back toward Manassas. A rear guard action was still being fought, but Lee had triumphed yet again, inflicting twice as many casualties as he suffered.

Nathan saw Billy sitting on a wagon hitch with his head down. When Nathan approached and called his name, the huge man slowly raised his head and looked at Nathan with haunted eyes. Over the next few minutes, he haltingly bore witness to his entire gun crew being killed when the cannon barrel burst. He had been at the rear of the caisson to bring up more shells and had been knocked to the ground by the concussion but was otherwise unharmed. He ashamedly pointed to a large dark stain on the front of his sack coat, blood, and brain matter from one of the crew. Nathan knew better than to try at that moment to convince Billy that he had nothing to be ashamed of. Instead, he sat on the hitch next to his friend and put an arm around his shoulder, and remained silent, watching men shuffle past from the battlefield.

Some days later, Abraham Lincoln sat at his desk in the White House, his head in his hands. His son Tad, now nine and dressed in a full-fitted officer's uniform for which he had hounded Lincoln for months, sat on the floor near the desk and contentedly set up pitched battles with small pewter soldiers. Lincoln hardly noticed the boy's presence. Earlier that morning his wife Mary had had another of her fits and had finally been calmed down by the White House doctor. She was now sleeping fitfully with the help of a laudanum draught. Lincoln was not happy about this treatment, but he trusted the doctor's advice. He worried about his wife's growing instability, and this added to pressing matters of state weighed immensely on him. Already in just over a year as president, his hair and beard were showing streaks of gray, and the creases in his homely face had grown deeper. And now the Union Army of the eastern theatre had suffered another defeat. What was he to do?

There was a series of sharp knocks on the office door, and Lincoln gave permission to enter. Secretary of War Edwin Stanton came in and walked purposefully up to Lincoln's desk, careful to avoid Tad's small military tableau on the floor. Lincoln could see by the intense look in the man's eyes and the muscles working in his jaw that he was agitated. Stanton cleared his throat which made his long beard waggle comically, and Lincoln suppressed a smile.

"Mr. President, we must come to a decision. The War Department is insistent that a change of leadership occurs at once."

Lincoln leaned back in his chair and looked at the secretary. "I suppose they think bringing George back is the answer."

"General McClellan seems the most logical choice at present, given his experience and his way of inspiring devotion in the troops."

"Those are certainly items to put in the plus column," Lincoln said slowly. "It's just that old George is so slow and cautious, I'm afraid that one of those tortoises studied by that Darwin fellow could very well beat him to the battlefield."

Ever the politician, Stanton chose his words carefully. "While General Mc-Clellan has at times presented some ... difficulties, we still believe that he is needed at this time to lead the Union army in this theatre, especially with reports that Lee may be planning to move north again."

"Are we hearing that from Pinkerton's group? If so, I'd take that information with at least a bushel of salt."

"Mr. President." Stanton's face had become flushed. He adjusted his small round eyeglasses. "We must have strong leadership in the field and quickly before that old grey fox outwits us again and ends up planting the Confederate flag on the White House lawn." His voice rose steadily in pitch as he spoke.

"Now hold on there, Mr. Stanton. Let's not give up the henhouse just yet." Lincoln scratched his beard and looked at the ceiling. Then he looked at Tad, who had stopped his play and was staring intently at him. Lincoln leaned slowly forward with a warm smile and said, "Tad, my boy, what would you do?"

Tad shot a quick glance at the secretary, who was muttering to himself and seemed only seconds away from wringing his hands, then looked back at his father. Trying to sound as adult as he possibly could, which made Lincoln smile all the more, he said confidently, "I believe that General McClellan is the best choice for the position."

"There you have it!" Lincoln slapped his enormous hands on the desk, startling the secretary. "I believe the captain here means what he says." He smiled benignly at the man in front of him.

Stanton looked puzzled. "So does that mean that we are reinstating General McClellan?"

"Yes, Mr. Secretary, it does. We will ride the tortoise and see if slow and steady actually wins the race."

"Uh, yes, Mr. President. I will inform the cabinet, and we will take all necessary steps to effect the change as expeditiously as possible." Stanton gave a slight bow from the waist and took a few steps backward, as if Lincoln were a potentate from olden times, before turning and exiting the office.

Lincoln looked at Tad with raised eyebrows, but the boy was already immersed again in his miniature battles. The President shook his head and chuckled. Though Stanton was at times a bit much to handle with his pride and correctness and bluster, Lincoln could not help but feel fondly for the old peacock. But as his mind turned toward the near future his chuckling died away. He turned his chair and looked out the window behind the desk, watching the soldiers and civilians walking to and fro on the streets in front of the White House. He sighed and murmured to himself, "General, what will you do for us this time around?"

Stanton was as good as his word. General Pope was removed from his command of the Union eastern forces and was reassigned to a post in Minnesota to deal with an escalating Indian problem. McClellan smugly resumed command and ordered a brand-new uniform for the occasion. To his credit, he appeared to refit his tired troops more quickly than in the past and got them on the move. Multiple intelligence sources had confirmed that Lee was definitely heading north, and

McClellan intended to show his handlers in Washington that he unquestionably deserved to be at the head of the Union forces.

Emboldened by his success in the most recent battle, Lee saw an opportunity to press his advantage while the command structure of the Union army was in transition. He also believed that he could shake Union confidence by invading the north, gain support from local populations, and even swell his ranks with new recruits to the Confederate cause. He further believed that further north lay an abundance of food for his hungry army. His target was Maryland, a politically divided state, and once he explained his vision to Confederate President Jefferson Davis, he was given permission to realize his plan. Unlike their counterparts in the north, Davis and Lee were building a solid working relationship. Though bouts of malaria had dimmed his physical eyesight over the years, the gaunt politician from Mississippi could see what he had in his silver-haired commander, and he was learning to trust Lee's judgment.

As the Army of Northern Virginia marched north, however, they were not given nearly the reception that Lee had hoped for. Though some Confederate flags hung from windows in rural Maryland towns, many citizens shut themselves indoors as the troops marched through. Worse still was the food situation. Having moved to the offensive after the Peninsula campaign, Lee's supply lines had grown longer by necessity, and these lines were now often broken or harassed by Union cavalry, which resulted in less food for his troops in the field. Marylanders offered little of their own supplies. Many a Confederate soldier raided apple orchards along the way and was unhappily surprised by loose bowels from the unripe fruit.

Nevertheless, Lee's army pushed on, eventually screening itself from the Union forces by a small range of mountains on their right flank. McClellan sent out cavalry to gather intelligence on Confederate positions but got little as a result. Lee drew up plans to push through gaps in the mountains and catch the Union troops strung out on the march. In a fortuitous stroke, his plans came into McClellan's possession when a private from an Indiana infantry regiment found a written copy wrapped around a bundle of cigars, lying on the ground at a crossroad. Rather than using the information to turn the tables on Lee, McClellan took a more defensive posture and consolidated his forces, matching the Confederate army's progress north toward the town of Sharpsburg.

The men of Company B, mostly veterans now, could feel a major engagement coming. There were the obvious signs. Shipments of ammunition, hard tack and salt pork increased. Officers were called to more meetings at headquarters. Cavalry units were on high alert and were sent off at all times of day or night. Pickets became skittish, shooting at everything and nothing. But beyond these signs was a sense of foreboding, a heaviness in the air. It was not a thing that veterans could explain, but they did pay attention to it. Every man had his rituals before battle, and they began to perform them now. Letters were written, muskets were obsessively cleaned, and Bibles were consulted for the first time in weeks or months. One man a few shelters down from Nathan and Christian turned his socks inside out, swearing on his mother's life that it gave him good luck. Chaplain Ericcson was certainly busier than usual. Men walked sheepishly to his tent with heads bowed and caps in their hands, looking for confession or forgiveness or just a word of encouragement.

On a clear night in mid-September, Nathan sat around a fire with several others. Earlier that day the company had drawn their usual marching rations of salt pork and hard tack, and also forty rounds of ammunition per man. Captain Shields informed them that their regiment would be stepping off early in the morning. Union cavalry had pushed Confederate pickets back on a solid body of gray and butternut infantry that afternoon near Antietam Creek, not far from their camp. Joseph Hooker's corps, of which the Pennsylvania regiment was a part, was to dislodge them from their positions. The company had been mostly quiet during supper. Now Nathan and his comrades in arms sat and stared into their fire, each with his own thoughts.

Far off in the distance, a banjo began to play a jaunty tune. Joshua stirred and looked off into the darkness. "I wonder if that's coming from the Rebel camp."

"My uncle told me a joke once about banjos," said Private Benizzio with a smirk. It goes like this: What's the difference between a banjo and an onion? Nobody cries when you chop up a banjo."

This drew a few chuckles and an apple core, which struck Benizzio in the forehead. The attacker, one Private Elijah Whittington from western Virginia, looked fixedly at Benizzio and said, "I'll have you know that my daddy is one of the best banjo players in the state."

Benizzio wiped apple juice off his forehead with a shirt sleeve. "Elijah, my sincere condolences."

Whittington shook his head as Billy guffawed and slapped Benizzio on the back. At that moment Chaplain Ericcson walked up to the circle. The men murmured greetings to him. He took off his hat and ran a hand through his thinning hair. "Good evening, men. I just wanted to wish you a pleasant sleep and God's blessings on you for tomorrow. May you be at peace knowing that He has you in

His hands." With that, he waved his hand over the group in a gesture of benediction, then walked away in the direction of another campfire.

Moments later Corporal Purvill stepped into the firelight. "Word from Sergeant Jeremiah: every man not on picket duty is to turn in now. We rise at four a.m."

With various groans and curses, the circle broke up and the men wandered off to their shelters.

5

JOSHUA WOKE WITH A start. A single candle flame flickered in a corner of the shelter, and by its light, Maxwell dug around in his knapsack and muttered to himself. Joshua sat up and rubbed his eyes. Maxwell turned and grunted, "Morning, lad. Time to be up and about."

Outside the shelter, it was completely dark, and from the darkness, Joshua could hear the sounds of an army coming awake. "No word from General Bragg this morning?"

"Too early. He probably still has his scruffy little head tucked under a wing."

The two men were quiet for the next few minutes as they squared away their bedrolls and gathered their equipment for the day. As they stood outside to buckle on their accouterments, Corporal Purvill walked past and quietly announced, "Hurry along, men. Make sure your cartridge boxes and cap pouches are full, as well as your canteens. Fall in as soon as you are able."

Maxwell called out to him. "No fife and drums this morning, Corporal?" Purvill spoke over his shoulder. "We're falling in quiet this morning, Private."

Gradually, the men of Company B filed into their ranks. Sergeant Jeremiah called them to attention and sized them, then called roll. Other than two men in the hospital with dysentery, all were present. With officers, they were eighty-one men. Captain Shields had the sergeants check muskets, cartridge boxes, and canteens. A detail was quickly sent off to fill canteens that needed it, and several men headed to the woods to relieve themselves. Then they waited.

Gradually, the dark gave way to the gray of dawn, accompanied by a thick fog. All around them were the murmurs of conversation in the ranks, punctuated by occasional laughter. They waited. Captain Shields ordered the men to stack their muskets and be at rest. He took out a watch he kept in a small vest pocket. At that moment a rooster crowed. Shields looked directly at Maxwell with a wry grin and said, "The general speaks."

This drew a wave of laughter from the ranks and a quiet "Huzzah!" from Private Maxwell. Suddenly, from the distance came the deep rumble of artillery. At first, it was desultory, but soon it swelled into a constant thunder. The men in the ranks grew quiet and restless. After a few minutes, an aide rode up on horseback and called for regimental officers to gather with him. There followed a brief meeting; then the officers returned to their units. Captain Shields called Company B to attention, had them take their muskets and load them, then ordered bayonets fixed. When this was done, he cleared his throat and said, "Gentlemen, as you can plainly hear, the ball has opened. We are one of the first regiments to go in. Good luck and God bless us all." Then he ordered, "Shoulder, arms. Left, face."

With practiced skill, the company shifted smoothly to a column of fours. Officers took their positions. Captain Shields stood a few paces ahead of the column and drew his sword. Before long the company ahead of them stepped off, and Shields gave the order to march. They walked along a narrow lane that cuts through a forest. The fog swirled around and over them, causing strange distortions to sounds in the distance. They marched up a slow rise and came out from the trees onto open ground. Joshua looked behind him and was awestruck by the vast blue column moving like an unstoppable river up the rise. The artillery fire became immediately louder. Joshua looked to his left and could see muted pink and yellow muzzle flashes from the Union guns. A slight breeze pushed the fog aside for a moment and revealed at least five batteries of four cannons each, almost wheel to wheel. The seven-man crews worked tirelessly to clean, load, aim, and fire their pieces with remarkable speed and precision. At the last cannon in line stood a giant figure holding a rammer. As Joshua watched, the man took off his cap with his free hand and waved it in the air shouting, "Give 'em hell, Pennsylvania!" It was unmistakably Billy.

Now the column approached a dense field of corn on their right, tall and green. Captains halted their companies and had them face front. Shields shouted to his men over the roar of the guns, "Stay tight to the man on either side of you!

I want no gaps! Guide on me!" He turned and gave the order to march and almost immediately disappeared from view when he stepped into the corn.

Joshua locked his eyes on Maxwell's thick neck directly in front of him. As soon as they got into the field all sound became muffled. The artillery stopped firing. All that could be heard was the crackling of corn stalks and the quiet cursing of men as they stumbled over the uneven ground. The corn was over their heads. The world was reduced to green, gray, blue, heavy breathing, and sweat. Captain Shields called a halt and the ranks tumbled together in confusion. He had them dress ranks and stand at rest while he and a lieutenant walked ahead.

Three files to the left of Joshua's position, Christian bent over to catch his breath and took a drink from his canteen. His heart was pounding with nervous energy, and it did not help that the chill and humid air was difficult to breathe. Just as he took another drink Captain Shields reappeared, his bedraggled lieutenant in tow. Shields called the company to attention, and they marched cautiously forward. After a few minutes, they emerged into a clearing where a swath of corn had been harvested. Shields halted them and called for quiet in the ranks, and they stood in the swirling fog, now tinted gold from the rising sun.

Christian strained with his eyes and ears for any sign of movement across the way, but for now, there was none. He began to relax and then, just at the edge of his hearing came the faint clinking of metal on metal. It slowly grew in strength, but the source remained out of sight.

Then, as if out of a nightmare, spectral shapes began to materialize out of the mist. Captain Shields drew his sword and turned with his mouth open, and suddenly hell broke loose from across the space with a roar and gouts of flame. Christian heard the sickening thud of lead smacking into the body of his file partner, and the man jerked backward and fell into him.

Shields gave the order to fire, and Company B answered with a tight volley. They loaded as the piercing Rebel yell reached their ears. Then they marched forward as balls whistled around them and more men began to fall. Shields halted them and gave the order to fire at will, and just as he finished, a body of Confederate infantry came crashing through the corn to their right. The unit on the right flank of Company B disintegrated under withering fire, the survivors stumbled back into Company B and then all was chaos. Shields ordered a retreat and went down with a bullet to the shoulder. The lieutenant looked at him with shock and suddenly his forehead disintegrated, and he fell face down.

Christian stood and loaded his musket as men all around him began to give in to panic. Christian brought the musket to his shoulder and looked for a target and felt a sharp sting in his right calf. He heard yells to his right and pivoted in that direction. At almost the same instant two hammer blows to his chest knocked the air out of his lungs. He staggered backward half a step and steadied himself with his left leg. Everything around him looked lighter. Sounds began to fade. The world tilted sideways, and he was lying on the ground. A corn stalk was jabbing into his temple, but he could not move. Suddenly, he thought of Rachael. He reached out a hand and tried to call her name. Tears came into his eyes. He felt himself being rolled over and a face appeared close to his own. He recognized the face but for a moment he could not remember the name attached to it. He blinked twice and then it came to him. Nathan. Nathan. Nathan . . . Then all went dark.

Nathan retreated into hell. He remembered nothing of the next several hours. When he finally came to, he was lying on a hospital cot with Joshua sitting next to him. With a worried face, Joshua told him how he had been dragged away from Christian's body, how he had not flinched when a bullet punched a hole through his thigh, how he had been carried back to camp in the middle of an insane and bloody firefight through the cornfield, which had cost the lives of three stretcher bearers, how he had not made a sound when the surgeon poured alcohol on his leg and stitched up his wound. All this Nathan heard with a faraway look in his eyes. When Joshua noticed after a few minutes and shook him gently by the shoulder, Nathan focused on Joshua's face and smiled faintly. Joshua talked further about horrific fighting around a sunken road and a bridge over Antietam Creek before twilight stole over the bloody fields and the two armies rested uneasily.

He began to talk of the losses to Company B when a soldier two cots away with a bayonet wound began screaming as a surgeon approached him holding a long metal probe. Two orderlies rushed to the cot and tried to hold him down, but the soldier kicked out and caught one of the orderlies in the face. Two unwounded soldiers came over to hold the man, and at that moment Joshua heard an unearthly wailing. He turned back to Nathan and saw a look of sheer terror on his face. His eyes were wild, and his mouth was impossibly wide open. With one hand he clenched the front of his shirt and with the other, he pointed to a spot above Joshua's head. His wailing grew louder as the other man shrieked and thrashed about. Other wounded soldiers began to stir and murmur. Joshua looked around in panic for an available surgeon or orderly, but none were to be had. In desperation, he turned back to Nathan and slapped his face. Nathan's expression did not change, and he wailed louder. Joshua slapped him again, harder. Nathan did not even blink. Finally, Joshua punched him hard enough to turn his head. The wailing died away, and Nathan closed his eyes for a moment. When he opened them again, he slowly turned and looked at Joshua, but his eyes were dead. The hairs on the back of Joshua's neck stood up as he whispered, "Nathan?"

By this time the soldier on the other cot had been sedated with chloroform and orderlies were quieting other wounded in the tent. Joshua motioned to a surgeon, a younger man with a kindly face, to come to Nathan's cot. Nathan continued staring in Joshua's direction until the surgeon snapped his fingers in front of Nathan's face. Slowly Nathan turned his gaze toward the surgeon, but nothing registered on his face. The surgeon looked worriedly at Joshua and then moved a finger across Nathan's field of vision and told Nathan to follow it with his eyes. Nathan did not move or speak. The surgeon sighed and bowed his head, then looked at Joshua and said quietly, "Come with me."

Joshua followed the surgeon out of one end of the tent. They stepped over dead and wounded soldiers lying haphazardly on the ground. Moans and cries filled the night air and set Joshua's teeth on edge. The surgeon led him into a small, wooded area that was relatively quiet, and stopped. He leaned against a tree and crossed his arms, murmuring mostly to himself, "I've never seen this many wounded before. We don't have enough surgeons or supplies for this. We just don't . . ."

"Sir," Joshua said with quiet desperation. "What is wrong with my brother?"

"I've seen it before. We don't know what to call it. It's as if the brain gets overwhelmed with too much horror and shuts a person away from it for a while, almost like protection."

"Will he come out of it?"

The surgeon shrugged. "I have no idea. I've seen some be fine after a few hours, and I've seen others descend into madness that looks as though it will keep them imprisoned until they die. It's a wonder it doesn't happen to more of these poor souls, with what they go through in these wretched battles," he said bitterly.

"What can we do?"

"In my experience, having them stay in a quiet and calm place for a while and treating them with kindness helps. And having people they know come visit them. Not so easy to do, though, with provosts prowling through the hospitals looking for stragglers or deserters."

"I don't understand."

The surgeon shook his head with disgust. "Men in this condition are considered cowards, doing anything they can to avoid battle. Officers, enlisted men, and even civilians treat these men with contempt. They think a man should be able to shake off the horrors of battle and go back for more without blinking an eye. I've seen soldiers dragged out of their hospital cots, beaten and spit on by men in their own units though their minds are clearly broken."

"I will not let that happen to my brother," Joshua said fiercely.

The young man smiled faintly. "I appreciate your heart, soldier, but I sincerely doubt your company commander will allow you to stay by your brother's side for an undetermined amount of time. Leave it to me. I may be able to find some hospital work for him to do once his wound heals."

"Thank you, sir. I appreciate it. I will look in on him when I can." Joshua turned and walked off.

The surgeon stayed where he was for a few more minutes, breathing in the night air. Then he straightened his shoulders and walked back toward the hospital tent and the carnage that awaited him there.

At roll call the next morning, Company B numbered thirty-four men including officers. Twenty-one men were known dead, eighteen were wounded, and eight were missing. Captain Shields wore a sling and looked older as he stood in front of his men. There was not much to tell them. Shields was not generally given to commending his soldiers for bravery or stirring them with patriotic rhetoric, and he did not do so now. He told them to look after their weapons and themselves, and to be ready to fall in at any time should the order be given to pursue the Confederates. He ordered sergeants to check ammunition in the ranks and report to the lieutenant, and he dismissed them.

There was light skirmishing the following day, in which Company B was not involved. It was initiated mostly by Lee as cover for his retreating army. The telegraph wires from Washington burned hot as the War Department urged McClellan to follow Lee and destroy him but McClellan demurred, citing high casualties and exhaustion. In truth, he had over twenty thousand troops in reserve that he had never committed to the battle, but again his extreme caution won out. The Confederate forces limped slowly back to Virginia, leaving nearly twelve thousand casualties behind. The Army of the Potomac had suffered roughly the same number, thus sadly marking this battle as the bloodiest single day of the war so far. Over the ruined fields lay a pall of smoke as soldiers dragged shattered wagons and dead horses into huge piles and burned them. Hundreds of blacks from the Union camps were put on burial detail. They wandered the ground holding shovels and lanterns, working far into the night with kerchiefs tied around their faces to keep out the stench of death.

Under the watchful eye of the young surgeon and a hard-working staff of volunteer nurses, Nathan's leg healed well. His wound was kept clean partly by allowing fly larvae to eat infected tissue in his leg, a treatment the surgeon had learned of in written accounts from doctors in Napoleon's army. The nurses had Nathan up and walking as soon as he had strength. Many others in the tent, however, were not so fortunate. Though the medical field had made great advances in recent years, much was still not known about treating shattered bones, abdominal wounds, or infections. Men by the dozens died quietly every day around Nathan as they succumbed to internal bleeding and sepsis. Some of the orderlies and nurses could not take the overwhelming tide of suffering and death and walked away. It was a testament to the iron will and dedication of the hospital staff that more did not do the same.

Rachael sat at her kitchen table, staring out the window. In her hand was a letter written by Joshua, telling her of Christian's death. Tears rolled down her cheeks and dripped from her chin onto the floor. Micah sat at her feet happily playing with wooden blocks. A tear dropped onto his head, and he glanced up at Rachael with a puzzled look. He cooed softly to her and reached out to touch her leg, but she did not register his presence. After a minute he focused again on the blocks, a thousand miles away from the grief that tore at his mother.

Though Nathan's leg was well on its way to healing, his mind was not. In the days following the battle, as the army around him licked its wounds and rested, he lay on his cot and stared into nothingness. When Joshua or one of the other men from Company B came to visit, he would sit up and hug his knees and not say a word. The surgeon looked in on him when he could and spoke encouragingly to him, but he knew that there was no medicine or surgery to heal the wound that could not be seen or explained. All he could do was wait and watch.

His reason to hope came from two unlikely sources. The first was Chaplain Ericcson, who visited Nathan every day with his Bible and a sweet, calming presence. He would hold Nathan's hand and read Scripture and talk softly by the hour, not seeming to care whether Nathan was engaged or not. When he was present Nathan became visibly more relaxed and his gaze seemed just a bit nearer, and for that the surgeon was grateful.

The other positive force that began to call Nathan back was a young Black orderly named Ezekiel, an escaped slave who had secured his freedom by offering his services in the hospital tents of the Union army. Whether he was carting off amputated limbs for disposal, emptying chamber pots, wiping up vomit, or enduring the complaints and racial slurs from wounded and unwounded soldiers alike, he invariably met it all with a smile and a nod. He had family down around Vicksburg, Mississippi, all working as slaves in the cotton fields, and he was convinced that one day they would be free with the help of God and "Mister Abraham's army." When others would ask him how he could remain so cheerful given the misery of his life, he would tell them simply that he was proud to serve his fellow men for a just cause.

Ezekiel took a special interest in Nathan from the first day Nathan was brought to the hospital tent. He would make it a point to stop at Nathan's cot every day and make sure he had enough food and water, and that his dressings were properly tended. When he had time, he would bring in a local newspaper and read to Nathan, a skill learned on his route along the Underground Railroad and gratefully shared. He always had an especially warm smile and a kind word for "Mister Nathan."

It was Ezekiel who came to Nathan several days after the battle with a smile that seemed to light up the entire tent. A soldier the next cot over with a serious chest wound coughed and spat up a thick wad of bloody phlegm, then said bitterly to Ezekiel, "What's got you so sunny today, darkie?"

Ezekiel turned and beamed at him. "The Year of Jubilee is comin'!"

"What nonsense are you talking about?"

"Mister Abraham just announced the Emancipation Proclamation! If the southern states don't stop fightin' by the end of this year, all the slaves in those states will be declared free startin' January 1 of next year, sir!"

The man shook his head gruffly. "Bah! Just 'cause Lincoln says it don't mean it's gonna happen. Now get me some water!"

"Happy to do it, sir." Ezekiel handed the man a canteen and turned back to Nathan. "Did you hear that, Mister Nathan? My family's gonna be free!" He leaned down and placed a hand gently on Nathan's shoulder. "It's been such a long time comin', but they're gonna be free, sure as heaven. Free!"

As he said the last word Nathan suddenly tilted his head and his eyes focused on Ezekiel's face. His mouth opened and at first, there were no words. Then he swallowed and whispered, "Free?"

Ezekiel's eyes went wide. "Did you just speak, Mister Nathan? Honest?" His eyes filled with tears, and they began to trickle down his cheeks. Nathan slowly reached out a hand and touched Ezekiel's face.

"Free?"

Ezekiel put his hand over Nathan's and began to laugh. "Hallelujah!" He gently turned and called out to a surgeon. "Sir! Mister Nathan just talked! Honest, he did!"

The surgeon walked over and began to examine Nathan. Ezekiel straightened and moved to the side of the cot, weeping with joy and murmuring, "Praise God! Looks like another slave on his way to bein' free."

To say that Nathan's recovery from that day was swift and sure would not have been true. In fact, it was barely the beginning. Over the next days and weeks, he often lapsed into dazed silence. Many nights he woke drenched in sweat, holding his pillow tightly to him and shouting Christian's name. Loud noises not only startled him but left him agitated for hours. And yet the kindness of Ezekiel and the chaplain and the hospital staff began ever so slowly to smooth the ragged edges of his terror. He started to read again, and to respond more when others spoke to him. The look in his eyes became less haunted.

Outside the hospital tent, events moved inexorably on. The War Department's insistence that McClellan pursue Lee's battered army was met with a steady stream of arguments and excuses from the general. Lincoln decided to visit McClellan's headquarters at Sharpsburg a few weeks after the battle, commemorated by a likeness taken with McClellan's staff, but even his personal appeal produced little effect. It was another few weeks before the Army of the Potomac finally began to gather itself together to move.

The young surgeon, a man named Fullerton, could sense the change as officers began to visit the tent more frequently to check the status of their men. When he saw the first provost walk in on a rainy morning, he went that hour to get consent from Captain Shields, then hurriedly dispatched a telegram to a colleague in Washington, DC, asking him to take Nathan on as an orderly in one of the hospitals there. He held the affirmative answer in his hand the very day a provost walked up to Nathan's cot and ordered him to stand. Nathan had had a miserable night of sleep, visited by terrifying images of Christian dying in his arms. It took him some time to rouse himself, and the provost became impatient and roughly grabbed his arm. "On your feet, soldier!"

Fullerton called out, "Sir!" and walked hurriedly to Nathan's side. "What is this man's condition?" the provost growled at him.

"Severe wound to the leg."

"Any infection?"

"No, sir."

"Can he walk?"

Fullerton sighed. "Yes, sir."

"Then this soldier has no business being here. He should return to his unit immediately."

"He has orders to report to a hospital in Washington as an orderly at the end of this week, sir." Fullerton held out the telegram.

The provost grabbed it and read it carefully. After a long moment, he glared at Nathan, then at the surgeon. "Seems fishy to me. We need men in the ranks, not changing dressings. Too many shirkers in this damned army." He let the telegram drop to the floor and walked away, mumbling under his breath.

Joshua and the chaplain visited Nathan the night before he was to leave, clasping his hand and wishing him good luck and Godspeed. The next morning Nathan sat nervously on his cot, waiting for an orderly to bring him to a nearby railroad hub. As he checked his bags for the hundredth time Ezekiel approached him with a serious expression.

"No smile today, Ezekiel?"

The old man looked at Nathan gravely. "Truth is, Mister Nathan, I'm gonna miss you." "I will miss you too, Ezekiel. You have been a great friend to me."

"I do believe that God's gonna look out for you, sir. You're one of my special ones." He paused and shuffled his feet, then reached into a trouser pocket and brought out a wrinkled and yellowed scrap of paper, roughly shaped like a butter-fly. He held it out to Nathan and said, "My mammy gave this to me some time ago, and it's always been special to me. I want you to have it."

Nathan shook his head. "I can't accept this, Ezekiel."

"Please, sir."

Reluctantly Nathan took it. One side was blank. When he turned it over in his hand, he saw some faint writing. Though it had faded with time, he could still make out the words, "For freedom Christ has set us free – Gal. 5:1." He looked up at Ezekiel, puzzled. "What does this mean?"

Now a smile began to steal over the old man's face. "It's a reminder, Mister Nathan. Look it up sometime."

"All right. But why a butterfly?"

"Ever seen a butterfly out in nature that didn't look free?"

An orderly walked up to Nathan's cot. Nathan smiled and stood. "No, Eze-kiel, I don't believe I have." He reached out and pulled the surprised man into a hug. "I will keep this with me always." He stepped back and looked into Ezekiel's eyes. "Watch out for yourself."

Ezekiel met Nathan's gaze. "God bless you and keep you, Mister Nathan. Maybe we'll be seein' each other again one day."

"I would like that." Nathan picked up his bags and followed the orderly. At the entrance, he turned back. Ezekiel had turned away and was propping up a man in his cot. Nathan saw Fullerton out of the corner of his eye and thought to walk back and thank him, but just then the surgeon picked up a bone saw and bent over a man on a table. Nathan said a silent thank you, squared his shoulders, and walked on.

The train ride to Washington was uneventful. The cars were mostly full of other soldiers, many of them wounded. Most kept to themselves, subdued by pain or laudanum or some inner thought. Nathan sat by himself most of the time, look-ing out the window at the turning leaves. The trip was somewhat longer than usual due to occasional line switches. One soldier who sat across the aisle from Nathan mentioned that Confederate cavalry had recently torn up sections of track on var-ious raids in the area, and it was taking some time to repair them. This explained why Nathan frequently noticed squadrons of Union cavalry riding parallel to the lines.

He had never been to the capital before, and the size and grandeur of the city impressed him. The streets teemed with carriages and well-dressed people. Sol-diers were everywhere, walking in groups or manning stout gun emplacements that ringed the city limits. White and gray marble buildings stood silent and imposing like judges. Nathan found himself sitting up straighter as these sights met his eyes.

Once he had disembarked, he approached a station master and showed him a letter from the hospital where he was assigned, asking for directions. The station master flagged down a carriage and said to the driver, "Harewood General Hospi-tal." Nathan boarded the carriage, and they were off, headed in a generally north-west direction. After about fifteen minutes, the carriage turned onto a long gravel drive that curved up a low hill. Nathan could see several outbuildings that looked like they belonged to a farm, and many canvas tents were being erected. The driver stopped at one such tent and with a slightly impatient tone informed Nathan that they had reached his destination. Nathan got out slowly, his leg still bothering him, paid the driver, and walked to the entrance of the tent.

Inside all was flurry and business. Surgeons and nurses and workmen talked over each other and waved papers. Nathan managed to catch the attention of one nurse and asked where he could find the hospital administrator. She pointed toward a distinguished older man with eyeglasses and a luxurious beard, bent over a small desk. Nathan made his way to the desk and said, "Excuse me, sir?"

After a moment the man looked up. "Yes?"

"I'm Nathan Butterfield. Dr. Fullerton sent me to this hospital to be an orderly." He handed the man a copy of the telegram that Fullerton had given him. The man looked at it and looked at the tent ceiling for a moment in thought, then brightened.

"Oh, yes. Chester Fullerton. Good man. Well, I can't say that I remember this particular telegram, but we can sure use more orderlies." He put out his hand. "Dr. Simon Morgenthal, hospital administrator." Nathan took his hand and was surprised at the iron grip. "As you can see, we're kind of a mess right now. We just opened about six weeks ago, and we are trying to get our ducks in a row to handle the increasing numbers of wounded." Morgenthal waved over an orderly. "Kindly take this man to Ward 6 and connect him with the head nurse there." The old doctor gave Nathan a wry grin. "I wish I could give each new staff person a personal tour, but unfortunately that is quite out of the question right now. I will try to look in on you when I can. And thank you, Mr. Butterfield, for coming to help us in a time of great need." Morgenthal bowed his head briefly toward Nathan, then turned to talk with a contractor who had been hovering at his elbow.

The orderly, a tall thin man who introduced himself as Crittenden, motioned to Nathan to follow him. They exited the tent and walked down a broad greenway between two long rows of tents and outbuildings. Crittenden explained that the land had indeed been a farm at one time, owned by a man named Corcoran and bought by the War Department recently. He stated that the hospital was being laid out in an open pavilion style, a relatively new concept in the city and being considered for other future hospitals. Eventually, they came to a long canvas tent with a hastily painted sign outside announcing it as Ward 6. Nathan followed Crittenden inside and found a nurse talking to several orderlies. When the conversation ended, Crittenden introduced her to Nathan and took his leave.

Nathan smiled at the woman and received a grim look in return. The woman in front of him was of middle age, short and solidly built with graying hair. Her blue eyes were piercing, and her posture was ramrod straight. The very air around her seemed to stand at attention. She took a moment to look at Nathan up and down, then said in a clear voice, "Mr. Butterfield, I am Nurse Hathaway. As long as you are at this hospital you will be under my supervision. I expect you to show up for work on time, neatly dressed, and not under the influence of substances. I expect you to be diligent in your duties and to follow directions without question. Do you have any questions before I give you a short tour?"

Nathan said softly, "No, ma'am."

"Very well then. By the way, are you related to General Butterfield of the Fifth Corps?" "Not that I'm aware of, ma'am."

"I see. Follow me." For the next several minutes, Nurse Hathaway showed Nathan around the ward, pointing out supply cabinets and nursing stations. She explained the various duties of the orderlies, from accompanying the wounded in wagons from docks on the Potomac and at the train stations, to securing their belongings, providing basic care, washing the wounded, reading to them, distributing mail, and stocking hospital supplies. Nathan would also be on a rotation for assisting in and cleaning up after surgeries, and burial detail. Nurse Hathaway consulted some papers at a desk near one end of the tent, wrote out an hourly schedule for Nathan, and gave it to him. He was to start the next morning. Before she dismissed him, she asked, "Do you have a place to stay in Washington, Mr. Butterfield?"

"No, ma'am."

She wrote down an address on another piece of paper and handed it to him. "My sister has a boarding house about fifteen minutes' walk from here. I'm sure she can put you up."

Nathan touched the brim of his cap. "Thank you, ma'am. I appreciate it."

He walked out of the tent and got directions from another orderly, and after a brisk walk found himself in front of a plain but well-cared-for two-story brick home. He knocked on the front door and was greeted by a woman who was the mirror image of Nurse Hathaway. Nathan introduced himself and explained that the nurse had sent him. The woman broke out in a warm smile and said, "Well, it is so nice to meet you, Mr. Butterfield. I am glad that my sister Eugenia sent you in my direction. I have a nice room available upstairs at the front of the house. Come in and take a look."

Nathan entered and immediately felt at home. The furnishings were adequate if not extravagant, and all was clean and orderly. He found the room upstairs to be rather small but comfortable. He asked about rates for room and board, and they seemed quite reasonable.

After a moment's thought he said, "Ms. Hathaway, I would like to stay here."

"Wonderful! I would love to have you, Mr. Butterfield. However, my last name is actually Mercer. Hathaway is my maiden name. Eugenia never married. She has dedicated herself to her work." She gave a wry little smile.

"And where is Mr. Mercer?"

"Dead, I'm afraid. Benjamin was killed some years ago in a railway accident, along with our only child."

"I'm sorry to hear it, Mrs. Mercer."

She cleared her throat and looked away for a moment. "Well, these things happen." When she turned back, she was smiling through tears. "But I have a new family now. Here in this house. There's old Colonel Posten and Mr. James, who is an orderly at another hospital, and the Shillings girl and her baby. You'll have a chance to get to know them in time, I'm sure."

Nathan settled into his new room that afternoon, enjoying the autumn sun coming in through the windows as he folded and put away his clothes in a modest dresser. Afterward, he took off his coat and boots and lay on the bed, realizing how tired he was from his travels. What seemed a second later, he was awakened by Mrs. Mercer knocking softly on his door, announcing that dinner would be served shortly. Nathan thanked her groggily and sat up, surprised at how deeply he had slept. He quickly washed with a pitcher of water, a bar of homemade soap, and a basin that was set on a small stand with a mirror in one corner. He took a quick look in the mirror and was surprised at how pale he was, after all his time campaigning in the fierce heat and sun of summer. He put on a clean shirt, wet and finger-combed his hair into some semblance of order, and headed downstairs.

The savory smells of roast beef and potatoes and bread greeted him as he stepped onto the main floor and turned to his left into the dining room. Already seated at the table was an old man with rosy cheeks and a neatly trimmed beard wearing an old flannel coat and a young girl in a plain dress who attended to a baby in a highchair next to her. Mrs. Mercer entered from the kitchen holding a beautifully done roast on a platter, surrounded by cooked vegetables. Nathan asked if she needed any help, and she shook her head graciously, setting the platter gently on the table and motioning him to sit. Nathan sat at the end of the table opposite Mrs. Mercer.

"Well, it appears that Mr. James is running a bit late, so I believe we will start." Mrs. Mercer folded her hands and the two others at the table immediately bowed their heads, familiar with the dinner time ritual of the house. Nathan bowed his head also and waited while Mrs. Mercer offered a short and earnest prayer. At its conclusion dishes were passed one at a time around the table. As they began to eat, the old man smiled warmly at Nathan and said, "Good evening, young man. Welcome to the Mercer house. I am Colonel Posten."

Nathan nodded a greeting and then shifted his glance to the young woman. She began to duck her head shyly, then looked at Mrs. Mercer who was watching her with motherly eyes. She sat up and looked at Nathan ever so briefly, murmuring softly, "Good evening. My name is Anna Shilling, and this," she motioned to the baby with a proud little smile, "is Bartholomew." Having said this, she quickly picked up a knife and fork and focused on her plate. Mrs. Mercer gave a satisfied smile and asked if anyone wanted coffee.

The conversation that evening was taken up largely by Colonel Posten, who seemed delighted to have a new audience. He spoke in great detail of land he owned in upstate New York, the fifth in succession of his family. He shared marvelous adventures he had experienced as a seaman on a British man o'war, battling the navies of "Old Bony" at the turn of the century. But his eyes glinted most brightly as he talked of his service under old Winfield Scott in the War of 1812.

"Now there was a commander," he said to Nathan with a sigh. "Made up his mind to do something and by Jove, he got it done!" He leaned toward Nathan with a conspiratorial air and whispered loudly, "You know, my boy, it was his Anaconda Plan that was adopted by the War Department at the beginning of this bloody shindig. I daresay if they stick to it and win the war, Old Winnie will have quite a feather in his cap." He winked at Mrs. Mercer and took a drink of wine.

Near the end of the meal, the front door opened, and a young man entered. He was tall and lean and had a confident air about him. He bowed briefly to Mrs. Mercer. "My apologies, ma'am.

They kept me long at the hospital today."

She waved his apology away. "I understand, Mr. James, and I appreciate your willingness to help our soldiers. Please join us."

The young man smiled. "I must beg off for now. I'm afraid I smell rather terrible from my work. I need a good wash, then I will fix myself a plate from the kitchen if that's all right with you."

"Perfectly fine, Mr. James. And may I introduce our new boarder, Mr. Butterfield."

Mr. James stepped forward and offered his hand. "Will James. Pleased to meet you." "Nathan Butterfield. Likewise."

"Well, if you will excuse me, I will retire to wash off the cares of the day." He nodded to the old man. "Colonel." Then he turned to the young woman and winked. "Anna." She blushed and dropped her eyes to her lap.

Nathan helped Mrs. Mercer clear the dishes and then went up to his room. He lit a lamp and started to write a letter to Rachael, but he could not find the words he wanted and grew restless. After a while, he gave up and set the letter aside. He took the lamp and walked downstairs.

Colonel Posten was dozing in a chair in the sitting room, and Anna and Mrs. Mercer were not in sight. Nathan ventured out to the front porch and sat in a rocking chair. It was a surprisingly mild evening and he breathed in the clean autumn air.

A few minutes later the front door opened, and Will came out, holding a plate of food in one hand and a glass of water in the other. He saw Nathan and stopped. "All right if I join you?"

"Fine by me."

Will sat on the porch railing opposite Nathan and set down his plate and glass. "Helluva day. Surgeon cut off the wrong leg on one patient, three men died of gangrene." He sighed and took a drink of water.

"Which hospital do you work in?"

"Armory Square. Been there ever since they opened up. How about you?" Nathan stood and stretched.

"Harewood. Just started there."

"How has it been so far?"

"Okay, I guess. A lot to learn."

Will took a bite of food and nodded. "Stick with the nurses. Some of them can be kind of crotchety, but they know their stuff. Clara Barton's training program is really making a difference." Will ate a bit more. "Seen any fighting?"

"I have."

"Whereabouts?"

"A few minor skirmishes. Peninsula campaign." Nathan hesitated. "And Antietam."

Will shook his head. "What a God-awful mess that was. I worked with a group of orderlies on the field. How did your unit make out?"

"We, uh . . ." Nathan swallowed. "We got hit pretty hard."

"Were you wounded?"

"In the leg."

Will looked at Nathan. "Taking a while to recover?"

"You might say that. Surgeon thought I could do some good here in the meantime."

Will held up a hand. "No ill will here, friend. I have nothing but respect for men who are willing to fight." He continued quietly. "I couldn't get myself to pick up a musket against another man, so I volunteered as an orderly. Even with that I've seen and heard my share of horrors."

Nathan stared at the floor. "Yep."

"For some reason, it's almost easier for me to deal with the screams of wounded men than horses." Will shuddered. "Those poor beautiful beasts out there hauling around men and guns, they're innocent in this fight. They get torn up and make those awful sounds until someone finally shoots them. I can't get that sound out of my head. And the smell of all the dead horses being burned—."

"Stop," Nathan said abruptly. Then more softly, "Please stop."

Will took a deep breath. "Sorry. I grew up on a horse farm not far from here, and it just makes me sick to see them suffer. I guess helping men is my way of trying to deal with it."

The two sat in silence while Will finished eating and then smoked a cigar. After a time, Nathan excused himself and went up to his room and laid down. Sleep eluded him for hours as bloody scenes paraded through his mind. He finally drifted into fitful dozing, waking more than once from a dream in which he was holding a dying Christian in his arms while the world went up in flames around them.

The next days and weeks saw Nathan settle into something of a routine. His days were busy at the hospital, learning the art and science of caring for the sick and wounded. He began to forge working relationships with some of the surgeons and nurses, and he learned that he could relate well with many of the men that came through the hospital. He would walk home exhausted but with a sense of fulfillment. As the weather grew colder, his leg ached more, but the warmth and hospitality of Mrs. Mercer's boarding house were usually all that was needed for that to fade into the background. Evenings were often spent with Will and the colonel, smoking cigars and trading stories of battles and foreign lands. Nathan also began to get acquainted with Anna just a bit, coaxing her into conversation with gentle words. Little Bartholomew became quite taken with Nathan and loved to sit on his lap while the adults talked. Little by little, Nathan's soul began to feel some peace.

One day at the hospital Nathan noticed a new orderly in his tent, sitting next to a cot and talking with one of the wounded. He had an unruly head and beard of graying hair, and his eyes were intense, but he spoke kindly and held the man's hand. Another orderly came up to Nathan and nudged him. "Do you know who that is?"

"No. Should I?"

"That's Walt Whitman."

Nathan had read a few selections from "Leaves of Grass" some years earlier. He had not told his father of this since the collection of poems had been widely criticized in Christian circles as too sensual. However, Nathan had been drawn to these works by their raw emotion and genuine expression of the common man. At this moment he felt shy and curious about the man at the same time.

His thoughts were interrupted by a nurse who sternly ordered him to take some fresh sheets to recently vacated beds at the far end of the tent. Nathan shook himself and went to a cupboard to retrieve them, and when he turned around with arms full, he saw Whitman standing in front of him. Nathan stood still and could think of nothing to say. The man's eyes were first curious, then impatient.

"Excuse me, young man. I need to get into that cupboard for some supplies."

Nathan mumbled an apology and stepped aside, then walked toward the empty beds with the sheets. As he made the beds, he glanced in Whitman's direction every once in a while. The man moved with energy and purpose, but otherwise, he seemed quite ordinary. One of the nurses told Nathan that Whitman moved from hospital to hospital in the area every few weeks with no fanfare or wish for attention, and he was a hard worker. Nathan wanted to speak to him, but the daily demands of hospital work kept them apart, and one day Whitman was gone.

Nathan wrote of the experience to Rachael and filed the experience away in his mind.

Not too far from the hospital, the offices of the War Department were in a flurry. Secretary Stanton and President Lincoln had finally had enough of George McClellan. Despite intense pressure from Washington to pursue Lee's wounded army after the draw at Antietam, McClellan had once again made excuses and barely moved. In November McClellan was replaced by Ambrose Burnside, the jovial and blustering general with glorious side whiskers whose division had been stymied at the Antietam Creek bridge. With great fanfare Burnside put the Army of the Potomac into motion, over 120,000 men strong, with plans to outrace Lee's army south to Richmond. Burnside's path led through the town of Fredericksburg, Virginia, on the Rappahannock River. He ordered pontoons and engineers to build a floating bridge across the river for his troops to cross. In this the War Department let him down, delaying the delivery of men and materiel for days due to bureaucratic inefficiency.

What happened next was one of the great tragedies of the war, fueled by foolish pride as was so often the case. Rather than adjusting to circumstances for the sake of speed Burnside chose to wait near the river for the pontoons to arrive, giving Lee a chance to dig in on the heights behind the town. Burnside's subordinates begged him to reconsider and offered alternative strategies for an attack, but Burnside would not hear of it, believing in his original plan and the strength of his army. The river crossing and initial push through the town seemed easy enough, though the engineers took heavy casualties. But Lee had prepared a murderous field of fire along the hills further back, and for three days Burnside fed his men piecemeal into a frozen killing field the war had not yet seen, before finally retreating with his shattered remnants back across the river.

Word of the slaughter began to trickle into Washington along with the wounded, whose numbers soon began to overwhelm the docks and train stations. Nathan was stationed at his ward as the casualties began to arrive, and the haunted looks on their faces made the hair on the back of his neck stand on end. At first, he was too busy to take in the horror these men had experienced. Surgeons and nurses had him running from one end of the tent to the other fetching supplies, carrying stretchers, and clearing space for the wounded to lie down, many on the ground as beds were quickly filled.

What caught his attention and began to disturb him was the number of men with frostbite. Throughout the battle, the weather had turned deadly cold, and even the well-clad Union soldiers could not long endure days of exposure on the freezing ground, unable to move due to the horrific fire from the Confederate lines. Nathan saw hundreds of blackened fingers and had to cut off boots frozen onto dead feet. After tearing the sack coat from a man's body and listening to his screams of pain as two orderlies held him down, Nathan could take it no more and walked outside the tent. He took deep breaths of frigid air and looked skyward, trying to push down the tide of panic rising inside him.

A nurse walked up and told him to go to a neighboring tent for bandages as Ward 6 was running low. Nathan took one more breath and began to walk to his left. He heard a familiar voice calling his name and turned. Sitting on the ground near him was Private Benizzio, a bandage around his neck and one arm ending in a ragged stump above the elbow. He motioned Nathan over with his other arm. "Nathan. Good to see you, man."

Nathan walked slowly over and kneeled down. "Benizzio. My God."

"Not a pretty sight, am I?" Benizzio winced. "Well, I don't have to worry about my missing fingers anymore. And strange to say, the cold actually saved my life. Froze my arm so I didn't bleed out."

"Has anyone looked at you yet?"

"No. I'm guessing there are men worse off than me." He stopped, and his face grew serious. "Maxfield is dead, and Whittington, and Purvill. Our company took it hard, Nathan. A lot of good men killed on those damn heights."

Nathan could hardly form the word. "Joshua?"

"I'm sorry, Nathan. I don't know. It was every man for himself out there. Had to hide under bodies to stop the bullets, units all mixed up—."

Nathan held up a hand. "It's all right. It's all right." He stood up. "We at least need to get you inside." He stood and held out a hand. Benizzio looked up at him and the familiar wry grin appeared.

"Sorry, my friend. My feet are blocks of ice. Probably lose them, too."

Nathan called over two men with an empty stretcher and directed them to take Benizzio to Ward 6. Benizzio grabbed his hand as they lifted him up. "Don't worry about me, Nathan. I'm too stubborn to die."

They walked away and Nathan stood for a moment, dizzy with fear. He knew this feeling from Antietam, a dark monster lurking in the shadows of his mind, growing stronger. As he walked to a nearby tent and asked for bandages, he could sense it trying to claw its way out. By the time he returned to his ward, he could barely breathe. He woodenly put the bandages in a cabinet and turned. A man lay on a cot next to the cabinet with a chest wound, muttering to himself. He saw Nathan and clutched at his sleeve. Their eyes locked, and Nathan could see the monster looking back at him.

"The sound . . . the sound . . ."

Nathan could feel himself starting to fall over the edge. With every ounce of strength he could muster, he wrestled a smile onto his face and bent over the wounded man. "Can I help you?"

"All night long, that sound. Slap. Slap. Slap. Bullets hitting meat. All around me, nowhere to go, that poor bastard laying in front of me." The man's voice went higher as hysteria began to creep in. "I used him. He couldn't feel it, right? I had to survive. I had to live."

"Sir, I think you need to—."

"I thought he was dead, he had to be dead, but then he moved!" The man was almost shrieking now. "How could I have done that? Use another man as a shield? My God!"

He went on, but Nathan was gone. The monster reared up and took him. His eyes saw nothing, and his ears heard nothing except a high-pitched whine. His body went rigid, he began to shake, then he fell into darkness.

He was in the family cabin. Seated at a long table were dozens of people eating and talking, from every season of his life: his family, the neighbor boys, Mr. Oversby, teaching colleagues from Kansas, and men from Company D. He looked through the dining room window and saw a massive tornado bearing down on the cabin—black and filled with swirling debris. He shouted in alarm and pointed outside, but the others only smiled at him and continued their conversations. A roaring filled his ears, and the cabin roof was torn off. One by one people were sucked up into the tornado, their napkins still in their laps and surprise on their faces. He looked to one end of the table and there stood his mother, wearing a blood-soaked nightgown. She smiled and spoke his name gently. "Nathan."

Somehow through the maelstrom, he could hear her, and he tried to answer but found he could not. She called to him again and again, and at last, she said, "It's all right, my son. Not yet." Then the scene faded to black.

He opened his eyes and found he was lying on a cot. Around him were the soft murmurs of hospital staff tending to their duties. It was mostly dark except for several lit lanterns hanging from ridge poles. He felt a cool sensation on his forehead and turned his head. Next to his cot sat a nurse, gently patting his face with a damp cloth. He could make out little of her features except for dark eyes and hair. She put the cloth down and smiled. "Well, there you are."

"What happened?"

"Surgeon said you had some kind of fit. You've been unconscious for a few hours."

Nathan tried to sit up, but the nurse put a firm hand on his shoulder and pushed him back down. "Not so fast, Mr. Butterfield. You need rest." Her voice was low and soft, with a lilt Nathan could not place.

"But my work—."

"Will wait. There are other orderlies. Rest now."

Something about her voice calmed him, and he settled back onto the cot. "What is your name?"

"Anna Maria Angelica Josefina Vittorio." He looked at her, puzzled. "You may call me Maria."

"Nathan."

She smiled and smoothed out the coverlet on his pillow. "Well, Nathan. Is there anything I can get you before you retire for the night?"

"Some water, please? To drink?"

"I'll be right back." She rose gracefully and walked over to a water barrel. She was tall and slender, and her shadow wavered in the lamplight. She returned with a cup of water which Nathan drank gratefully. When he finished, he realized he needed to relieve himself. Maria called over a male orderly and together, they helped him to his feet and supported him as he walked shakily to the sinks. When he had finished, they helped him back to his cot and tucked him in. He asked for another blanket and Maria brought one. As she leaned over to cover him her hair brushed his cheek, and Nathan caught the clean scent of lavender. She turned down the lamp closest to his cot and bid him good night.

Nathan lay awake for some time, aware of nurses moving around him and men breathing heavily in medicated slumber. Very slowly, he drifted off into sleep and woke what seemed seconds later drenched in sweat. Maria sat beside him holding his hand. "You had a bad dream, Nathan. You are safe. I'm here with you." He looked at the outlines of her face in the lamplight as his panicked breathing slowed. The warmth of her hand gave him peace. After a time, he slept again, and this time he rested well.

In the morning when he woke, Maria was gone. He could not remember what he had dreamed of the night before and was glad of it. An orderly brought some oatmeal, and he thought of the dark-haired nurse as he ate. He was helped to the sink after breakfast and felt a bit stronger. The air outside the tent was brisk and fresh, and he breathed in deeply. He was beginning to feel that the world would be all right again until he reentered the tent, and the smell of rotting flesh assaulted his nose. His eyes watered and he gagged. He found it hard to breathe and the tent began to spin. The orderly with him said, "Easy, Mr. Butterfield," and helped him quickly to his cot. He laid down and pulled the blankets over his head and succumbed to the terror in his brain.

Later, he heard a soft feminine voice calling to him. He felt a hand on his shoulder and flinched. The voice called to him again. It was Maria. "Nathan. I'm here with you." He lay still and said nothing. "Nathan. You don't have to come out right now. I will be right here when you're ready."

The terrible smell was less noxious under the blankets, but he wanted to see her face. Slowly he pushed back the blankets until he could see around him. Maria sat in a chair next to him, and in the morning light, her face was like an angel. She smiled and her warm brown eyes glowed with compassion. He reached out, and she took his hand. He sighed, "I'm glad you're here."

"And I will be here for a while, Nathan. Now, what is bothering you?"

"The smell. Dead flesh." He shuddered.

"It's all around us, isn't it? Frostbite, gangrene, amputations. It brings back horrible memories, yes?"

"I can't get them out of my head."

"They will stay with you for a long time."

Nathan sat up and held his nose. "I can't live the rest of my life like this. I'm a soldier, for God's sake."

She looked at him fiercely. "And this is your battle for now. To deal with these fears until you beat them into submission."

"I am a coward—."

"No!" She pointed a finger at him, and her eyes were blazing. "It is a lie to think that a man can look on the horrors you have seen and be at peace. The mind can only take so much."

"But other soldiers have seen what I've seen, and they are still fighting."

"They have found a way to lie to themselves, to put away the terror for now. But it will come out one day. It will always come out." She put both of her hands on his and spoke gently. "I have worked in the asylums of France. I have seen men and women reclaim their minds and their lives with the proper help. I have hope for you, Nathan. I will see you through."

He wanted to believe her, with all his heart he wanted to, but the terror seemed like an unassailable force pressing on his sanity. Weakly he said, "What about the smell?"

"Ah!" She held up a finger and dug in a bag at her feet. She produced a small tin and took off the lid. Immediately, a powerful scent like pine trees hit Nathan's senses and he moved his head back. "Camphor!" she said triumphantly. "We'll put a dab of this under your nose every day to drown out the other smells."

His eyes watered. "For how long?"

"Until you don't need it anymore."

Something in her eyes told him that he could trust her. She gave him a small, confident nod, and he nodded back shyly. She dipped into the tin and gently rubbed a small bit of the camphor on his upper lip. His nostrils nearly burned with the scent, but he could no longer smell rotting flesh. His heart and his breathing began to slow. He looked gratefully at Maria. "I think it's helping."

"Good. Now rest, and we will talk about more steps to take later. I will leave the camphor with you. Don't use too much." She gave him a wink and a smile and put the tin on a small table by Nathan's cot. She rose and walked toward a small group of nurses at one end of the tent and began a conversation with them, occasionally looking back at Nathan as she talked. Nathan lay back on his cot and breathed in the camphor, picturing tall pine trees like sentinels swaying in the breeze by the cabin.

Over the next several days, Maria developed a structure for Nathan. Each morning after breakfast, he would walk with an orderly around the hospital grounds, weather permitting. Then he would do light chores around the ward, a little more each day. If the panic began to rise up in him, he would sit on his cot and focus on a candle flame for several minutes while breathing slowly. In the evenings' Maria would come and talk with him for a little while. He learned that she was from Italy and had come to New York to stay with a cousin just before the war broke out. He learned that her father was a mandolin maker in the small town where she was born, and he and her mother still lived in the same house on the bank of a river. Nathan learned that Maria was one of eight children, some of whom still lived in Italy, and she had wanted to be a nurse since she was a little girl. He learned that she had been engaged at one time, but her fiancée grew restless with rural life and one day announced that he was moving to Rome to seek his fortune, and she never heard from him again.

Maria coaxed Nathan to talk about himself as well, and he began to share details of his life with her. He found her easy to talk to, and a good listener. He felt safe with her, and he looked forward more and more to their time together.

One morning Nathan came back from his walk and found a small commotion in the ward. A tall figure with a stovepipe hat was standing in the main aisle surrounded by several armed soldiers. It was Lincoln. Nathan was stunned to see how much the man's face had aged in the years since Nathan had seen him. He watched quietly while the president removed his hat and gestured for the soldiers to wait at the entrance to the tent. Then he walked to a cot on which lay a soldier with a heavily bandaged head. Lincoln sat on a chair next to the cot and began talking gently to him, nodding and smiling as the man struggled to form a few words. After a time, Lincoln shook the man's hand and Nathan distinctly heard him say, "Thank you." Then he rose and walked a bit further down the aisle and sat with another soldier.

Nathan began his orderly duties, but he often stole glances at the president. The great leader seemed in no hurry. He went from cot to cot and gave each man his full attention, asking about who he was and his experiences in the war. And always at the end of each conversation, there were quiet and humble thanks. Eventually, Lincoln finished his visits with the men and spoke briefly with a surgeon. He bowed awkwardly to the head nurse, patted an orderly on the back, and left with his detail. Nathan watched him go, grateful that such a man occupied the highest office in the land.

Less fulfilling tasks awaited the president at his office on Pennsylvania Avenue. Almost since the outset of the conflict, the governments of France and England had shown various levels of interest on both sides, ranging from business negotiations to carefully worded outrage over American naval aggression. Ambassadors from both nations, particularly England, flitted around the capital like moths, trying to gain attention and favor from Lincoln and his cabinet. When Lincoln arrived at his office that day, he was told by his secretary that the British ambassador was waiting to see him. Lincoln gave the secretary a grim look and directed him to track down the American ambassador or some other official from the State Department to meet with the British diplomat instead. Then he walked to another office by a back way and sat in quiet, waiting for War Secretary Stanton to find him. He guessed he would be left in peace for five minutes, and it was not much later that he heard the quiet knock on the door.

Stanton entered, his beard and face long as usual. He was here to talk about the perpetual thorn in the side of the War Department, military command. The latest chapter in this saga was Ambrose Burnside. The bewhiskered general was noticeably less jovial these days, having amassed a shocking number of casualties at Fredericksburg under his leadership and now dealing with supply problems. These two factors had caused morale in the ranks to plummet, and desertions were on the rise. In addition, Burnside had lost little of his stubbornness through the recent campaign. Apparently taking a page from McClellan's manual, he was resisting pressure from Washington to pull the army together and get moving again, citing an all too familiar list of concerns and complaints. Lincoln stared silently at the Christmas decorations in the office while Stanton's beard wagged with outrage. Finally, he held up a hand and Stanton grew quiet.

"When I was a boy, my father knew a man in town who kept pigs. He had one old boar who was particularly stubborn, and so this man devised a system in which he would hit this pig with larger and larger sticks until finally, the pig would move."

Stanton harrumphed. "Mr. President, I fail to see what that provincial anecdote has to do with General Burnside."

"Mr. Stanton, I believe it is time for us to use a bigger stick."

While Lincoln and the War Department debated how best to motivate their errant general, things continued to move apace at the hospital. Nathan continued his daily routine and gradually felt his inner terror begin to recede. His feelings of gratitude for Maria's care began to evolve into something more, and he found himself wanting to be with her as much as possible and yet feeling shy around her. When they were together, he would search her face for some sign that she perhaps felt something deeper for him as well, but he did not trust his interpretations. He wanted to tell her his feelings but was afraid that he would chase her away if he did so. He drank in the sight of her raven hair, the touch of her hand, the clean smell of her, and he felt frozen. He became frustrated with himself.

A few days before Christmas, he received a letter from Rachael which provided a temporary distraction from his thoughts. Rachael was full of news about her writing (a few more of her essays had been published), Micah (now walking and getting into everything he shouldn't), and Ezra (still not talking, moving a bit, his eyes as fierce as ever). She wished Nathan a Merry Christmas and asked him to write her as soon as possible. He read the letter three times and each time felt sadder and more alone.

Though Mrs. Mercer promised a lavish Christmas meal and perhaps a present or two, Nathan was not feeling the joy of the season and volunteered to work two shifts at the hospital on Christmas Day. This decision was received with gratitude from the administrator and tight-lipped skepticism from the head nurse, who thought Nathan was already working too much as it was. He shrugged this off and got to work, making his usual rounds with the wounded. He had hoped that Maria would be there but at the last moment, she had decided to accept an invitation from her cousin to spend a few days with her in New York City. Nathan did his best to show some cheer as he brought special meals to those who could eat. He read a letter from home to a young artilleryman who had lost his sight from a burst cannon barrel. He read excerpts from Dickens' beloved Christmas story to another man who had never learned to read. A small group of men and women from the Christian Commission stopped in and sang several carols and hymns. When they had finished, they handed out small New Testaments to men who wanted them and prayed fervently for their bodies and souls. This occurred near the end of Nathan's shift and drove him into a dark and somber mood. He barely acknowledged the cheery yuletide wishes from the staff as he put on his greatcoat and walked out into the night.

A chill wind blew as he made his way to the boarding house, accompanied by occasional snow flurries that swirled along the streets. Nathan hunched his shoulders and trudged through the darkness as memories of past Christmases flowed through his mind. When he arrived at the boarding house, he found it mostly dark and quiet, but Anna was walking circles in the dining room with a fussy Bartholomew in her arms. When Nathan came in, the little boy stretched out his chubby arms to him, and Anna guiltily and gratefully handed him over. While Nathan spoke in low tones to the youngster, Anna went to the kitchen to fix him a plate of leftovers. When she came back to the dining room, her son was fast asleep in Nathan's arms, his fingers curled around Nathan's hair. Anna gently extricated the boy from Nathan and laid him on a couch in the parlor, tucking a blanket around him. She sat with Nathan at the dining room table while he ate, listening as he spoke of the events of the day. When he asked her about the festivities at the boarding house and of her childhood Christmases, she spoke haltingly but more than usual. Nathan enjoyed the conversation but could feel exhaustion setting in and excused himself for the night. Anna gathered his dishes and gave his arm a grateful squeeze as he walked toward the stairway. He fell asleep a few minutes after getting into bed.

Though his routine remained basically unchanged over the next several weeks, the same could not be said for the Army of the Potomac. At last, pried loose from inactivity by carefully worded pressure from the War Department, Burnside gathered his army for another campaign to bring the Grey Fox to bay, but this time weather and organizational incompetence conspired against him, and the troops became bogged down on the Virginia roads in early January 1863 in what would become known derisively as the Great Mud March. To be fair, Burnside had cautioned against a massive movement in winter, but as the commander of the army, the blame fell squarely on his sloping shoulders, and in late January, he was replaced by Joseph Hooker. In addition to having earned a reputation as a hard-drinking ladies' man, Hooker had shown himself a capable and aggressive commander at the division and corps levels in several major battles, and the War Department felt the Army of the Potomac was in dire need of such leadership at this time. Hooker wasted little time in putting his unique stamp on the Army of the Potomac, making wholesale changes at all levels of command and introducing corps badges to help build pride and esprit de corps among the various units. Drilling and refitting were once again the order of the day, and once again the rank and file were asked to raise their hopes for ultimate victory as they looked toward the south.

For the first time in many months, Nathan's heart was light. As the days passed in Washington, the relationship between him and Maria grew. They worked closely together on shifts at the ward, and sometimes when he looked up from a task, he found her looking at him appraisingly with her soft brown eyes. The head nurse noticed the growing feelings between them and pretended to disapprove, but she was secretly fond of both and saw the good of young romance amid all the darkness and horror, so one day she casually mentioned to Nathan that there were currently no male suitors pursuing Maria. Nathan's heart leaped at the news, and he thought of the pretty young nurse all the more. He tried to act calm when he was near her, but women have always known men's feelings for them, and Maria was no exception. Nathan's nervous chatter and awkward silences and shaking hands betrayed him, and this only endeared him to her more. Secretly, she hoped that he would make his feelings known to her, but she knew to be patient and to carefully encourage him.

Mrs. Mercer was bringing clean towels to Nathan's room one day and found him pacing and muttering to himself. Though she guessed from his demeanor that a woman was the cause, she feigned innocence and asked him what was on his mind. Nathan had thought of her as a kind and caring mother almost from the first moment he met her, and so now he sat on his bed and poured out his heart to her: He was falling in love with a nurse from the ward, he believed but was not sure that she might also have feelings for him, and he wanted to talk with her about it but did not know how to have a conversation like that. After several minutes of breathless speech, Nathan stopped and noticed the older woman gazing at him warmly. She walked over to the bed and sat beside him, reached over, and patted his hand.

"Nathan, I have watched you over these last months. I have seen how you are with the others here; I have heard how you speak of your family and the patients under your care. You have a good heart, and I believe you have love in it to share.

If this woman has even a few wits about her, she will see that you are a good man, and she will take you into her heart."

Nathan looked into her eyes for a moment. "But what if she doesn't feel the same way I do?"

"Are you worried about looking like a fool?"

He sighed. "Yes. I just don't have . . . experience in this kind of thing."

"Well, you are not the first." Mrs. Mercer chuckled softly. "Mr. Mercer was an absolute bundle of awkward nerves when he started courting me. I practically had to hang a sign around my neck saying that I was interested in him. Poor thing." She shook her head and chuckled again.

"How will I know what to say?"

"Say what's in your heart. Say it as honestly as you can. It doesn't have to be perfect, just genuine. If you do that, she will see your heart through all the bumbling and stumbling there may be."

Nathan rubbed his head. "Why does this feel like the hardest thing I've ever done?"

"If it didn't, I would be worried about you, my boy." Mrs. Mercer smiled and rose. "I know it makes you anxious, but I think you should talk to her soon. You never know what the future holds, and if you keep this inside you, I'm afraid you're going to fret yourself to an early grave."

Sleep eluded him for a long time that night, and when he finally fell asleep, he dreamed of chasing a wild horse, almost but never quite catching it. When he woke in the morning, he vowed to talk to Maria that very day, though the thought caused a cold feeling in his stomach. He dressed and ate quickly, glancing a few times at Mrs. Mercer who glanced back with a twinkle in her eye.

Outside, it was snowing heavily. Nathan trudged and slipped his way through the streets, rehearsing what he would say to Maria and trying to anticipate her response. He soon gave up trying to calm his nerves and used the nervous energy to propel him through the swirling white and the wind.

When he got to the hospital, he looked for Maria but was quickly directed by one of the nurses to shovel pathways between the tents. When he was done with that, he helped unload wagons of medical supplies and canned food that had just arrived. By the time he finished he was soaking and shivering, and the head nurse took pity on him and had him sit by a stove with a cup of hot coffee. When she brought him a blanket, he asked her if Maria was working that day, trying to sound as casual as possible. The nurse smiled to herself and informed him that Maria had been delayed by the weather and most likely would not be in until tomorrow. Nathan nodded, disappointment settling over him like dusk. For the rest of the shift, he went about his duties somewhat woodenly, putting on a brave face and willing himself to focus his thoughts on other things.

It proved a nearly impossible task, but after some time, the cold feeling left his stomach and work took over his mind. When his shift ended, he checked out with the head nurse and bundled up, noting that it was still snowing quite hard. He walked out of the tent and leaned into the wind, thinking of the warmth of the boarding house and a delicious dinner. He rounded the corner of a tent and ran headfirst into a tall slender figure, who cried out and fell backward into a snow drift. Nathan recoiled in shock, then stepped forward quickly and offered his hand. He could not tell who it was at first because the face was wrapped in a scarf and a hat was pulled far down on the head. But as the figure rose a lock of long brown hair escaped from under the hat and Nathan looked into brown eyes, and his heart fluttered like a captured bird. It was Maria.

Nathan stammered an apology and tried to brush her off. She began to graciously protest and then put a hand to her nose and discovered it was bleeding. Nathan was mortified and sheepishly guided her to a nearby tent, where he found her a place by a stove and hurried to find a cloth for her. When he returned, she had unwrapped her face and taken off her hat. She sat in the lamplight with bedraggled hair and rosy cheeks, dabbing at her nose as her eyes watered. Nathan had never felt for her more keenly.

Eventually, the bleeding stopped. Nathan asked her for at least the seventh time if she wanted coffee. She smiled and for the seventh time gently said no. She motioned him to sit, and he lowered himself onto a nearby empty cot. He was so happy and so embarrassed that he could not speak for a bit. Finally, he opened his mouth and said, "You're here." Immediately, he felt even more like an idiot, if that was possible.

She looked at him with dancing eyes. "I am. And quite a greeting you gave me."

"I am so sorry, Maria. I couldn't see and—."

"Nathan, it's all right. I will be just fine."

"Are you sure? Do you want me to get a doctor to—."

She put a hand on his arm. "There is no need. Others in this tent need a doctor far more than me."

Helpless, he fell silent. He looked at her in the flickering shadows and felt that his heart would burst out of his chest. He saw her looking at him, the expression on her lovely face changing from amusement to warmth and then something more. His embarrassment faded away. The staff moved around them as if in a graceful waltz. The two sat in their own little world for long moments. Then slowly, ever so slowly, they became aware again of the sights and sounds in the tent. Maria dropped her eyes and tucked a wayward strand of hair behind an ear. Nathan breathed slowly and found courage waiting for him. He leaned forward and took Maria's hand and said, "Would you have dinner with me at the boarding house tonight?"

Her eyes grew wide with happy surprise, then just as quickly they faded. "Oh, Nathan, I am scheduled to work in the ward tonight."

She stopped short at the sound of a small cough behind her. The head nurse had been watching the pair since they had come in and as Maria caught her eye, she winked and shook her head imperceptibly. Then she quickly put on a stern expression and approached them. She took Maria's face in her calloused hands and gazed intently at her nose. Then she stuck out her chin and with a slight Irish brogue pronounced, "Well, young lady, I'm afraid you're in no state to work this evening."

"But—."

"No ifs, ands, or buts, missy. You need to go and get some rest, straightaway." The nurse looked at Nathan with an appraising eye. "Perhaps this gentleman would be so good as to escort you." She turned back to Maria. "Which ward are you assigned to?"

The woman's gaze was so fierce that Maria was cowed and barely whispered, "Six."

"Right. I will inform the head nurse of that ward, and arrangements will be made to cover your shift. Now, bundle up well and be careful on the way." When Nathan and Maria looked at her with open mouths, she took hold of her apron and shook it at them. "Off with you two!"

Nathan looked at Maria and shrugged happily. She smiled and began to button her coat. In short order, they were on their way. The nurse watched them go with a twinkle in her eye. She was basking in a memory many years ago in Galway, during the Great Famine, when a handsome and very nervous young man had stood on the doorstep of her father's house with his hat in his hand, come to try his hand at courting her. With a contented little sigh, she closed the door on that thought and turned back to her work.

The walk to the boarding house would have been magical if the snow had not been blowing in their faces. As it was, they hunched into their coats and leaned into the wind. It was fortunate that Nathan was so familiar with the way, else they could easily have gotten lost. They saw no one on the streets, and most of the lamps had gone out. Nathan walked in front, hoping to block some of the wind. There was a warmth in his chest despite the weather, and whenever he turned to see how Maria was faring, the warmth grew a little more.

Eventually, they came to the boarding house and Nathan ushered her inside. They stood in the front hall shaking off the snow and unbundling themselves. Will was in the drawing room reading a newspaper. When the two came in, he looked over the top of the paper and assessed the situation, gave Nathan a wink, and returned to his reading. Mrs. Mercer came out of the kitchen followed by wisps of steam. Her rosy cheeks glistened in the lamplight.

"Well, Nathan. I see you made it safe and sound. That is a relief." She turned to Maria with eyebrows raised. "And who have you brought with you?"

Nathan hung up his greatcoat and reached for Maria's wrap. "Mrs. Mercer, this is Maria. She works with me at the ward."

Mrs. Mercer bowed slightly and smiled. "Well, Maria, it is a pleasure to meet you. Welcome to my boarding house."

Maria returned the smile. "Thank you so much, Mrs. Mercer. You have a lovely home." "Thank you, dear. It is made lovely by the people who are in it."

Nathan cleared his throat. "Mrs. Mercer, would it be all right with you if Maria stayed for supper?"

"There is always room at my table, Nathan. Please, come in and get warm. I will be ready to serve before too long."

Nathan and Maria took seats in the drawing room and Will put aside his paper. They talked pleasantly about their work in the different hospitals until Colonel Posten walked in. He bowed and kissed Maria's hand and promptly turned the conversation to himself. Halfway through a rousing tale of an Atlantic voyage, Mrs. Mercer called from the dining room that supper was served. As they were seating themselves, Anna walked in with Bartholomew in her arms. She curtsied shyly when introduced to Maria, and the little boy buried his head in his mother's shoulder.

The food and the conversation that evening were excellent. Nathan was grateful for the efforts made by the others to help Maria feel welcome. He was also impressed by her grace in engaging with the group around the table. She charmed the colonel with her attention to his wandering stories, she held her own with Will regarding political opinions, and she gently coaxed Anna out of her shell a bit. To Mrs. Mercer's questions about herself, she gave forthright answers. Even Bartholomew seemed taken with her, sneaking glances at her with his big brown eyes throughout the meal as his mother tried to get him to eat something.

After the meal, Anna excused herself to give Bartholomew a bath and put him down to sleep. Mrs. Mercer cheerfully rejected all offers from the rest to help clean up, and she walked toward the kitchen with her arms full of dishes, humming a country dance tune from her younger days. As she reached the door she turned back to Nathan and gave him a knowing smile.

The group settled again in the drawing room, and Colonel Posten started in on another story. Will and Nathan exchanged glances and after a few minutes, Will stood. "Colonel, would you care for a glass of port in the library?"

The old man's eyes brightened. "Ah, capital idea, my boy. Capital!" He stood as well and turned to Nathan with a broad smile. "Care to join us, Butterfield?"

Before Nathan had a chance to answer, Will had a firm hand on the colonel's back, steering him firmly toward the library.

Now they were alone. Nathan rose and put more wood on the fire, then sat in a chair closer to Maria. She settled back in her seat and closed her eyes. "Mrs. Mercer is a wonderful cook."

"Yes, she is. Would you like a blanket?"

"No, thank you. The fire is wonderfully warm."

Nathan listened to the wind howling around the corners of the house. "I don't think you should go home tonight." Suddenly, he sat up straight and began to blush. "I didn't mean - ."

Maria rescued him with a sly smile. "Mr. Butterfield, the only thing I heard in that statement is chivalry."

He breathed a sigh of relief, but now he was unsettled and lapsed into silence. They both stared into the flames for a time. Eventually, Maria stirred and said, "Tell me more about your family."

Haltingly at first, Nathan shared news from his sister's recent letter. Then he talked about his brother's work in the hospital system. Maria asked questions about his earlier years and Nathan told her of his schooling, Mr. Oversby's encouragement to try teaching, and his experiences in Kansas. She did not ask about his experiences in the war. She knew from experience that a man would not talk of such things until and unless he was ready. She did ask after Ezra and quickly realized that theirs was a complicated relationship. But she was gentle and skillful in her questioning and her listening, and Nathan found himself sharing thoughts and feelings with her that had been long buried. Some time passed before he realized that he had been talking at length, and he stopped and looked at her. Her eyes were fixed steadily on him, and he could not read the expression on her face. At that moment Mrs. Mercer breezed into the room.

"Well, Maria, I will not hear of you going home tonight. I am sure that Nathan would be pleased to offer his room to you."

Nathan nodded. "By all means."

Maria smiled. "I am grateful, Mrs. Mercer. I must admit, I was not looking forward to walking home."

"So, that is settled. Give me a few minutes to put fresh sheets on the bed, and then you can retire whenever you please." The old woman gave a quick nod and walked toward the stairs.

The two settled back into their chairs and watched flames mellow into embers. Nathan felt relaxed and alert, soaking in the moments spent with this woman. At first, he cast about in his mind for things to say, but he soon decided that nothing needed to be said. The clock in the hallway chimed the hour of eleven and Maria stirred.

"I think I need to get to bed. I can hardly keep my eyes open." She rose gracefully and touched Nathan on the shoulder as she passed. "Thank you for a wonderful evening, Nathan." At the bottom of the stairs, she turned and gave him a warm smile. "Good night."

"Good night, Maria." His words felt as though they were coming from someone else. He could still feel her hand on his shoulder. He sat for a while longer, happier than he had felt in a very long time. Eventually, he stretched out on a couch in the library with a blanket over him and tried to sleep, but his heart was beating fast. He could not wait to see her again. He closed his eyes and saw her hair shining in the firelight, hearing the warmth of her voice. He was spellbound.

He woke to the sounds of Colonel Posten rifling through a stack of magazines on a table near the couch and muttering to himself. He sat up and stretched. The colonel turned. "Sorry, young man. Didn't mean to disturb."

Nathan waved him off. "No harm done, Colonel. What time is it?"

"Shortly after six. Never could sleep late. Habits of being in the service and all that." "Is it still snowing?"

"I haven't looked, dear boy. I've been trying to find a *Harper's Weekly* from last month. Capital article on the British opinion of our blockade." He lapsed back into muttering and returned to his search.

Nathan rose and pulled aside the curtains. Snow lay thick on the ground and still fell heavily. On the street, he could see carriages struggling to make headway. He wondered how the staff at the hospital were getting on.

Suddenly, the events of the last evening flooded back into his mind. He turned quickly and started toward the stairs and then remembered that Maria was in his room. He looked at a mirror in the hallway and saw his rumpled state. In a panic, he walked to the kitchen and found Mrs. Mercer gathering pots and pans for the breakfast meal. She saw the look on his face and smiled. "Nathan, feel free to use the bathroom in my room to wash up."

He nodded gratefully and made his way there. He quickly washed and straightened his hair the best he could. As he walked back out, he saw some photographs on Mrs. Mercer's dresser. He stopped to look at them and was struck by an image of Mr. Mercer, standing tall and looking confidently at the camera, a closely cropped beard giving him an air of authority.

Nathan wondered if he would ever feel as self-possessed as the man before him appeared.

His head was bowed in thought as he rounded the banister of the stairs and bumped into a figure coming down. He staggered back a step with a quick apology and found himself staring into the laughing eyes of Maria. She tapped him playfully on the shoulder and said, "Well, Mr. Butterfield, we need to stop meeting like this."

For a moment he could not speak as his heart jumped into his throat. Then he took a deep breath and bowed gallantly. "Ms. Vittorio, it is an honor to run into you again."

She giggled and stepped to the main floor, taking his arm as they walked into the dining room. Soon the others assembled, and Mrs. Mercer began to bring out the food. As they ate there was much talk of the snowstorm and what it could mean for the functioning of the city. Nathan heard little of the conversation as he stole glances at the beautiful woman across from him.

Several times she returned his glance with unarming frankness. The meal concluded. Will and the colonel retired to the library while Nathan helped Mrs. Mercer clear the dishes. Maria followed Anna and Bartholomew into the drawing room. When Mrs. Mercer finally shooed Nathan out of the kitchen with the friendly flap of a dish towel, he walked to the drawing room to find Maria sitting on the floor stacking blocks with the little boy, chatting with Anna as she did so. His heart warmed to see how easily she got on with the others here. He leaned against the door frame and watched the scene contentedly.

Several minutes later there was a knock on the front door. Mrs. Mercer answered it and found a young hospital orderly who touched his cap and asked for Nathan. When he saw Nathan he said, "Mr. Butterfield, I've been sent by the ward nurse at Harewood to bring you and Ms. Vittorio to the ward. I have a sleigh." He gestured toward the street.

Nathan and Maria exchanged glances. Mrs. Mercer motioned the young man inside. "Come on in, sir. I'll get you a cup of coffee while these two get ready." The orderly stamped his feet and gratefully stepped into the foyer. Nathan and Maria set about dressing for the day and bundled up in coats and scarves. With heartfelt thanks from Maria to Mrs. Mercer, they were off, trudging through snow that reached to their knees. A strong mare shook her head impatiently as they climbed aboard the sleigh. The orderly handed Nathan a blanket and took his seat. Nathan and Maria tucked the blanket around them, and the orderly gave the reins a flick.

The ride to the hospital took some time as the sleigh had to weave around several carriages that became stuck in ruts and drifts. Twice the young man stopped to help free carriages, motioning Nathan to stay where he was. Nathan did so with only a slight twinge of guilt, savoring as he did the warmth of the blanket and the company of the woman beside him. They talked little, and it did not matter.

Finally, they arrived at the hospital and found chaos. Several tents had collapsed due to the weight of the snowfall, and the grounds were a flurry of nurses and orderlies moving the sick and wounded to temporary shelters while the tents were set back up. Nathan and Maria wasted no time jumping into the fray. Time passed quickly as their shift duties were necessarily multiplied. By evening both were exhausted and there was still much work to do. The ward nurse asked for volunteers to stay longer to help. Nathan raised his hand and saw that Maria did the same. Those who chose to stay were given a few minutes to rest and drink coffee and eat something. Then it was time to work again.

It was almost midnight when the last of the tents was back in order and the sick and wounded were bedded down. The snow had slowed to gentle flurries, and it had grown colder. Nathan could hardly keep his eyes open. The ward nurse found a teamster with an empty wagon who was heading in the direction of the boarding house. Nathan quickly scanned the ward and did not see Maria. The nurse thanked Nathan and told him that he needn't come to the hospital tomorrow. Nathan nodded tiredly and followed the teamster to his wagon.

If Nathan hadn't been so utterly spent, he might have found conversation with this man interesting. He had never heard someone cuss so much and so colorfully, and his stories of bringing supplies to the army in all conditions were the stuff of legend. Nevertheless, soon after climbing into the wagon, Nathan fell asleep. What seemed a second later, a hand was shaking him awake. The teamster was leaning over him, tobacco and whiskey strong on his breath.

Nathan sat up and blinked. He thanked the man and got down stiffly from the wagon. The teamster nodded and barked at his mules, then began a scratchy rendition of a song about a whore named Sally as he pulled away.

Nathan could barely remember trudging up the walk and into the house, taking off his coat and boots, and heading up to his room. When he lay his head on his pillow, there was a lingering scent of Maria there, but this barely registered before he fell fast asleep. He did not wake until late the next morning. He was sore, and his brain felt muddled. With a sigh he rolled out of bed and splashed water on his face, marshaling his energy for another day at the hospital. Halfway down the stairs, it blessedly occurred to him that he had a day off.

Mrs. Mercer found him in the drawing room talking with Will. She offered to make him a late breakfast, but he respectfully declined. Will had invited him to go to the Smithsonian Institution to view an exhibition of oil paintings of American Indians, and the two were keen to head out as soon as possible. Nathan quickly drank a cup of coffee, stuffed some biscuits in his coat pockets, and set off with Will.

They were within reasonable walking distance of the castle-like structure. Fortunately, the weather was fairly mild, and they took their time viewing the sights of the bustling city. Both quickly noticed the increased fortifications, evidence of a nervous administration, which had grown to fear the might and wiles of Lee's army.

There were not many visitors to the museum that day. The recent snows had slowed the city down. Nathan and Will found themselves almost alone. The paintings, by artist John Mix Stanley, were magnificent in color and detail. Nathan was immediately drawn to them. His mind went back to his journey home from Kansas. The stories he had heard from teaching colleagues and townspeople of murdering savages did not align with the noble people depicted on these canvases. They stood before him fiercely and proudly, their dark eyes looking to the future even as their gorgeous robes and jewelry bespoke a rich tradition. Both men were surprised when several hours had passed.

They realized they were hungry and found a small inn near the Smithsonian that was serving lunch. For the next hour, they ate and talked. Nathan learned that Will had some Mohawk blood on his mother's side. Will had been fascinated by Indians ever since he was given a copy of Cooper's book *The Last of the Mohicans*, from a relative who had been a missionary among the Sauk nation. Nathan told him of his distant sightings of Indians on his trip east. They mused out loud what it would be like to live with these people. Eventually, their talk wound down and they made their way back to the boarding house, with tales to tell at the supper table.

Nathan saw Maria two days later, hurrying toward a tent with her arms full of bandages. He thought of calling out to her but was content instead to watch her. Her cheeks were rosy from the cold and wisps of hair danced around her face as she walked. He felt an intense desire to hold her, to take her face in his hands and look into her eyes. His thoughts were interrupted by an orderly who whistled to him to take one end of a stretcher. He sighed and looked back toward Maria, but she was out of sight. He vowed to find her as soon as he could and ask her to take a walk with him.

He was placed on surgery duty that day. Over time, he had learned to steel his mind through these days of holding men down as they screamed in fear and agony, carting amputated limbs to burn pits on the grounds, and pulling sheets over the dead. But with the steeling came a price. His soul shrank. God became a distant, uncaring figure. At the end of such days, Nathan became remote, pulled into some quiet part of himself.

Today was no different. At the end of his shift, he sat on a wooden box outside the ward tent, staring at his boots. He absently wiped at a bloody handprint on his apron from the last surgery of the day, a boy of seventeen who had died pleading to see his mother. Nathan sat empty.

And then she was there, standing over him. He looked up at her and her lovely smile faded. "Nathan, what is it?"

He had no words at first. He shook his head slowly. Maria kneeled in the snow and took his hands, her face filled with concern. She opened her mouth to say something and then saw the handprint on his apron. Without a word, she found another box and put it next to Nathan, and sat with him in silence. After a few minutes, Nathan stirred and seemed to come awake. He took a deep breath and said softly, "Will you walk with me?"

She nodded. They stood and she took his arm, and they walked slowly among the tents until they reached a road. They wandered by the light of gas lamps in the twilight, saying nothing. Eventually, Maria grew cold and said she wanted to go home. At the steps to her apartment, she gave him a quick kiss on the cheek and wished him a good night. Nathan apologized for not being good company and walked home.

He slept surprisingly well that night, and when he awoke, he felt refreshed. When he saw Maria at the ward that day, he screwed up his courage and asked her to have supper with him that night. She had made plans to meet with a friend, but she quickly said that her calendar was open the following evening. Nathan walked home almost floating off the ground.

They took a carriage to a lovely little inn not far from the hospital. Will had lent Nathan a newer suit and the collar was uncomfortable, but he did not care. He could hardly take his eyes off Maria. She had styled her hair in a lovely braid, she wore just a hint of makeup, and her simple dress accented her color and her figure magnificently. When the carriage arrived at her apartment later that evening, Nathan helped her down and stood awkwardly with her at her door. Finally, he took her hand and kissed it; she gave him a coy little smile and curtsied and went inside. His heart was aflame.

In the days and weeks that followed, they saw much of each other, taking in the sights of the capital. As the winter faded into spring, they took to walking through the parks, talking and laughing. One evening they took a path along the Potomac and stopped beneath a majestic oak tree. As the sun glinted off the mighty river, Nathan stepped toward Maria, and she lifted her face to his. Her lips were soft and on her breath was a hint of sweet lemon. He took her in his arms, and they kissed for several minutes until they were startled by a deer leaping across the path close to them. They both laughed; then Nathan kissed her gently on the forehead. She nestled into his arms, and they watched the sunset on the water.

Nathan could not remember being happier in his life. Everything around him seemed brighter, sweeter, and easier. The work at the hospital was no less grueling, but the sight of Maria instantly lifted his spirits and made the work more bearable. Their time together gave life to him. He felt understood and accepted by this woman. At the same time, she seemed confident in herself and did not worship him. She was warm and funny and honest. She truly listened to him. Her touch calmed him. He did not know what he had done to deserve this gift, but he was grateful for it. And in his turn, Nathan did all he could to make Maria feel cherished and special.

He picked small bunches of wildflowers for her on his walks to the hospital. He wrote small notes and scraps of poetry for her. He told her often how beautiful she was. His embraces were gentle and firm. He thought that things could not possibly be any better until the day he told her that he loved her, and with tears in her eyes, she answered that she loved him.

It was so difficult for Nathan to focus at work after this that the head nurse had to take him aside and give him a stern lecture. Maria watched this with a smile and loved him all the more. To so captivate the heart of a man was heady stuff. But she knew that she must attend to her hospital duties well for the sake of the patients. More importantly, she knew that she needed to care for Nathan's heart well, and she wanted to. She saw in him a good man who could become better with love and encouragement.

Nathan was deep in thought one day at the hospital about how best to ask for Maria's hand when he heard a familiar voice behind him. His brother stood near the entrance of the tent. He was gaunt and had a few weeks' growth of beard. He raised his hand in greeting. Nathan asked the head nurse for a few minutes, and she nodded curtly. He walked to Joshua and hugged him warmly. "It is good to see you, brother!"

Joshua returned the embrace. "You too, Nathan." He stepped back and looked at him. "It seems that city life agrees with you."

"Yes, I believe it does." Nathan appraised his brother. "You, on the other hand, look like you've been starved and stomped on by a mule." He smiled and clapped Joshua on the shoulder. "What brings you to the capital?"

"We have a new colonel for our regiment, and he's recalling every soldier that he possibly can to fill up the ranks." Joshua stopped for a moment. "As you probably know, we've had some rough handling of late."

Nathan's smile was gone. "Yes. I saw Benizzio some months back. He told me about Fredericksburg. My God, it must have been horrible."

"There are no words." Joshua looked about the tent. "How is the little bed bug, anyway?" "Dead. Gangrene took him."

Joshua sighed. "So many gone. Nathan, you would not recognize our company anymore. Lots of raw recruits and only a few of the old faces left."

"I believe it is the same with most of the units."

"Well, I need to speak with the hospital administrator, deal with the paperwork, and all that. Can I see you when your shift is done?"

"Yes."

Joshua handed him a slip of paper with an address on it. "I'm staying at an inn on the other side of town. Meet me there and we can have supper and catch up." Joshua touched the bill of his cap and then pointed to his sleeve, where three bright yellow chevrons stood out against his faded sack coat. "I must be off. No rest for us noncommissioned officers."

Nathan smiled. "Well, Sergeant Butterfield. I guess the War Department is scraping the bottom of the barrel."

Joshua returned the smile. "Desperate times, brother. I'll see you for supper."

Nathan watched him go and suddenly thoughts of Maria flooded his mind. She was not on duty that day, in fact, was out of town visiting relatives, so he had no way to tell her this news today. She would be back in a day or two, and this was not the kind of information to share by telegraph. He returned to his duties with an unsettled heart.

When his shift ended, he hurried home and cleaned up, quickly told Mrs. Mercer that he would not be at her table for supper, then took a carriage to the inn where Joshua was staying. It was a small, plain house near the docks. Joshua met him on the porch, and they walked down the street to a restaurant that Nathan had not been to before. "Not much to look at, but the food is good and plentiful," explained his brother on the way.

They were served their food and drink rather quickly by a stout, middle-aged woman who was missing several teeth and winked suggestively at them several times. The two exchanged wry glances and then began to eat and talk.

Joshua mentioned that the new colonel was a West Pointer who did most things by the book and believed wholeheartedly in drill, much to the dismay of the rank and file. The regiment had seen no significant action since the Fredericksburg debacle, but there were now stirrings that a new offensive was afoot. Hooker was increasing pressure on the War Department for men and materiel, and the veterans knew what this meant. As to the specifics of the new plan, Joshua could not say. "But" he whispered after a sip of beer, "I'm pretty sure he's going to try to steal a march on old Lee. He'll want to make some points with the gentlemen in Washington after Burnside."

"And what news from home? I haven't gotten a letter from Rachael in a while."

Joshua shrugged. "Father seems to be holding his own. Micah is growing like a weed. More men from town are joining up, and a new state regiment is forming. And how about you? How is work at the hospital going?"

"It is a grind, to be honest. Our surgeons are competent, and we have an excellent nursing staff, but sometimes we get overwhelmed with the numbers."

Joshua shook his head. "If we could get some commanders who were half as competent as your surgeons and nurses, we might not be losing as many men."

"Are Shields and Jeremiah still there?"

"Yes, thank God. I swear sometimes they are the saving grace of our regiment. I'm surprised they haven't been promoted." Joshua took another drink of beer. "So, what do you do with your time when you're not at the hospital."

"Well, I have a friend who stays at the boarding house where I am, and we have seen some of the sights around here."

Joshua leaned forward. "Any women of note in your life?"

"Yes," Nathan said and blushed.

"Oho! Don't hold out on me, brother!"

Nathan took a breath. "Her name is Maria. She is a nurse on my ward." Nathan paused. "Joshua, she is the most beautiful woman I have ever seen. I love her and I mean to marry her someday."

Joshua sat up. "Lincoln's beard! My brother in love? Thinking of marriage?" A look of mock concern came over his face and he felt Nathan's forehead. "Have you caught a fever?"

Nathan chuckled. "I know. Who would have thought it? What I know about women and courting could fill a thimble." His eyes sparkled. "I would love for you to meet her."

"Well, by the colonel's orders, we are to set out for the regiment tomorrow." Nathan's face fell.

"She won't be back by then. How can I say goodbye to her?"

"Can you send her word through your hospital staff?"

"Well, yes, but—."

Joshua shook his head. "I'm sorry, but I'm afraid that's the best we can do."

There was little conversation after that. They finished their meal and said good night, agreeing to meet at the docks in the morning to begin their journey back to the regiment.

Two days later, Maria returned to her room in the city and found an envelope waiting for her on her bed. She put down her bags and picked up the envelope and her heart fluttered. On the front was her name written in Nathan's strong hand. She sat on the bed and took out a single sheet of paper. She took a breath and began to read.

My darling Maria,

I am on my way back to my regiment. While you were away, Joshua was sent to bring me back. It seems our new colonel wants to fill out our ranks once again, possibly in preparation for a new offensive.

My heart was broken that I had to leave before I could see you again. I long to hold you in my arms, to feel your softness and your warmth, and to hear the beauty of your voice. I miss you so much already that I find it hard to breathe. My mind and my heart are full of you.

I promise to write you as often as I can. I do not know when I will be able to visit, but as long as you think of me, I will be wherever you go.

With all the love I have to give, Nathan

Maria sat on her bed with tears streaming down her lovely face. Gently she pressed the letter to her lips and whispered, "With all the love I have to give."

6

THEY TOOK A STEAMER down the Potomac with other soldiers from various regiments. Some miles south the river made a great bend to the east, and there they disembarked and were put on train cars that moved them west toward Fredericksburg. With the help of a provost marshal, Nathan and Joshua finally located their regiment which was stationed on Marye Heights, just beyond the town.

The walk up the sloping ground was sobering. Hastily dug graves were everywhere, as were discarded muskets and accouterments. Many of the trees had been shattered by cannon fire. Nathan could not begin to imagine the carnage these fields had seen. He looked over at Joshua. His brother walked grimly, his eyes straight ahead and his jaw clenched.

They reached a stone wall below the crown of the heights, pockmarked and cracked all along its length but mainly intact. Just beyond the wall, Nathan caught sight of a familiar figure, small and ramrod straight, barking orders to a corporal. Nathan and Joshua approached quietly before Sergeant Jeremiah sent the man off and turned to see them. He nodded to Joshua and extended a hand to Nathan. "Good to have you back, son."

"Sergeant."

"Our company is bivouacked on the other side of these heights. Follow Corporal Savage, the man I was just talking to, and he will show you where and help you get settled."

He nodded to them and walked off. Nathan and Joshua followed the corporal, a tall man with a limp until they reached the company encampment. Everywhere Nathan looked were faces he did not recognize. They set up their shelter in numb silence. When they were done, they sat on the ground and took their boots off. Several minutes later a tall shadow fell over them. They looked up and saw the smiling face of the chaplain. They moved to stand but he gently held up his hand. "No need to get up on my account, gentlemen. I just came to welcome back Private Butterfield."

Nathan nodded. "Thank you, sir." "How was your time in Washington?"

"Interesting, sir."

"So sorry to hear about Private Benizzio. A bit rough around the edges, but a good man nonetheless."

"Yes, sir."

"Well, I imagine you're tired after your trip, so I will let you rest. God bless you for helping the sick and wounded, Private. Important work that will not be forgotten." The chaplain bowed slightly and left.

Night fell on the encampment. Joshua introduced Nathan to a number of the newer men, and Nathan made an effort to be cordial, but he was bone-tired. After a short time sitting at a campfire, he excused himself and laid down in the shelter. He wished for sleep but for a long time, it would not come. He pictured Maria's lovely face lit by sunlight, and he longed for her. Finally, he drifted off, calling her name in his mind.

The next days and weeks were filled with the drudgery of camp life. Nathan wrote to Maria as often as he could and waited for letters from her. He learned from company officers that General Hooker had amassed and set in motion an enormous force, and had indeed surprised Lee by traveling south faster than the Confederate commander had expected. Hooker's plan was to beat Lee to Richmond, or at least draw him out in pursuit and fight him on the ground of Hooker's choosing. He left several divisions behind near Fredericksburg to block any attempt by Lee to bring reinforcements from the east. In the event Lee did not do this, Hooker had a sizeable reserve to use as needed. This group busied itself by digging in and building fortifications facing west. And they waited.

Nathan came back from a day of digging absolutely exhausted. His back and arms were throbbing, and his hands could barely grip. He threw himself on his blanket in the shelter and put an arm over his face. Joshua came by a few minutes later. "Hey, Lazy Bones. Mail call."

"I don't care."

"Really?" Joshua nudged him with the toe of his boot. "What if there's a letter from your lady love?"

Nathan groaned. "Be a pard and bring it back for me." Joshua bowed low. "As you wish, my liege."

A few minutes later Joshua returned and dropped a letter on Nathan's chest. Nathan sat up and looked at Joshua, who had his hand extended. "Tip, sir?"

Nathan growled, "Get out of here before I 'tip' you with my bayonet."

Joshua chuckled and moved off. Nathan opened the letter and moved to find better light. It was indeed from Maria, and he read it eagerly. She said that she missed him greatly and was sorry she had not been able to see him off. She noted that work at the hospital continued as usual.

Then, to Nathan's dismay, she mentioned that she was thinking of joining a team of nurses under Clara Barton closer to the front lines, where more lives could possibly be saved. The famous nurse had visited the hospitals in Washington asking for volunteers, and her vision of work near the battlefields was so compelling that Maria could think of little else. She closed by confirming her deep love for Nathan, and her wish that they would soon be reunited.

Nathan was quiet at supper that night. When Joshua noticed and asked him, Nathan haltingly told him of Maria's plan. Joshua clapped him on the shoulder. "No field commander is going to put nurses in harm's way."

"How do you know that? Battle lines change quickly, artillery fire gets misdirected, there are cavalry raids . . ."

"So, tell her not to go."

Nathan snorted. "You haven't met this woman, brother. I might as well try to tell the earth to stop spinning."

Joshua smiled and wagged a finger at him. "What have you got yourself mixed up in, Nathan?"

"I honestly don't know." Nathan ran a hand through his hair. "I do know that I love her, and now I won't be able to stop worrying about her."

"Poor Nathan."

Nathan sighed. "Yes, poor me."

Early the following week orders came for the regiment's division to pack up and march west. They were to act as a rear guard when Hooker's main force passed by and to guard supply trains and telegraph lines against harassing Confederate cavalry. They left one morning in a drizzle that steadily increased as they marched, turning the roads into mud. The land west of Fredericksburg quickly became a dense forest, crowding up to the very edge of the roads. After several miles, the bedraggled troops were halted and ordered to encamp as best they could in the surrounding woods. Pickets were set out in all four directions, Nathan's company among them. He spent a miserable watch hunched up in his poncho under an ancient oak tree, straining his eyes to see anything in the inky darkness. At three in the morning, he heard footsteps approaching him. He called out the sign and received the countersign, exchanging places with a fresh-faced private who looked as though he would skedaddle any second. The corporal who came with the young man instructed him to stay alert and report anything suspicious to him, stationed fifty yards to his right. With that, Nathan made his way cautiously through the underbrush and at last found his shelter. He took off his poncho, laid down with a grateful sigh, and was asleep within a few minutes.

The dawn came clear and cold and with it the deep rumble of battle to the west. The men of Company D came out of their shelters and were greeted by a strange sight. Three large balloons hung in the air perhaps a mile distant, with long ropes hanging down below the tree line. A lieutenant stood near the mess tent looking at them through a telescope, and after a minute, Nathan saluted and asked if he could take a turn. The lieutenant, a recent graduate from West Point, looked him up and down and then reluctantly handed the instrument to Nathan. "One minute, Private."

"Yes, sir." Nathan held the telescope to his eye and scanned the horizon until he had the balloons in sight. He focused on the nearest of the three, watching with fascination as the men in the wicker basket beneath the balloon stared through field glasses and then leaned over and shouted down toward the ground. Every once in a while, they would duck, and Nathan imagined they provided a very tempting target. He felt a tap on his shoulder and handed the glass back to the lieutenant. "What are they doing, sir?"

"Reporting troop movements and such. I wouldn't want that job for triple my pay." The man smirked and returned to his viewing.

All day long the distant sounds of battle could be heard at the camp, muffled though they were by the dense forest. The men of Company D heard no solid details and could only watch as couriers rode in and out with dispatches. As the day wore on, the temperature dropped, and low clouds crept up from the southwest. By the time the men bedded down for the night, a slow drizzle had begun. This turned into freezing rain and when the camp awoke in the morning, there was a dusting of snow on the ground.

With the advent of daylight, the battle sounds resumed, and still, there was little word as to how either side was faring. Company D was again given picket duty and was spread out through the woods to the west of the encampment. As the sun rose, it became warmer and the snow on the ground disappeared. The distant clatter of musket fire was accompanied by a steady dripping from the trees.

Nathan was marched to a picket post at noon. He could barely see Joshua to his left in the gloom. The man on his right, a new recruit named Knowles, asked Nathan a few questions but when Nathan did not offer much in the way of a response, he eventually gave up and fell silent.

The woods grew warmer, and Nathan began to feel drowsy.

Suddenly, he came alert as he heard something crashing through the undergrowth perhaps fifty yards in front of him. He brought his musket to the ready position and shouted, "Who goes there?" He heard no answering voice, only the crashing sounds coming closer. He brought the musket to his shoulder and cocked it. "Answer me or I'll shoot!" The man to his right fired a shot that ricocheted off several trees.

"Hold up! Stop firing, for God's sake!" A Union soldier emerged from behind a tree with his hands above his head. His sack coat was torn, and there was a wild look in his eyes. Several other men trailed behind him, two of them slightly wounded. "We're 11th Corps."

Nathan brought his musket down. "What's the story back there?"

Instead of stopping, the men continued to stagger through the underbrush and went right past him. The last man in line turned and shouted back over his shoulder. "You'll get out of here if you know what's good for you!"

Joshua came toward him. "What on earth is going on?" Knowles walked up and Joshua barked at him, "You need to use your head out here! " Knowles lowered his eyes and leaned against a tree.

All around them now, men were emerging from the woods. There were no intact units or officers visible, only small knots of men streaming past them, driven by panic. A sergeant from Company D appeared behind Joshua and motioned for them to return to camp. As they walked into a small clearing, a major on horseback rode out in front and drew his pistol, shouting to the men to turn and rally on him. One soldier slowed long enough to spit at him. The rest went relentlessly on.

Nathan had never seen the like of this. On all sides of him, men jostled and pushed each other along, panting and stumbling in their hurry. Other than the occasional curse when one or another tripped and fell, there was no talking. The frenzied river of men carried them all the way to their camp, and they had to fight their way out of the current. The retreat kept on, leaving in its wake a trail of discarded muskets and blankets and haversacks. Eventually, Shields moved the company north a few hundred yards where the chaotic traffic was thinner. There they halted while Shields tried to find the colonel and get orders.

It took several hours for the division to get sorted out from the general mess. Finally, some order was restored, and they were marched westward to take part in a rear-guard action. Company D saw only light skirmishing and suffered few casualties. Eventually, they bedded down near an inn that sat at a crossroads, with pickets on high alert. Through much of the night, there was scattered small arms fire to their front, the Confederates probing the Union lines to see if there was more mischief to be done.

At least three significant stories emerged from this battle that was eventually to be called Chancellorsville, after the inn's owner. One was Lee's strategic brilliance put on display yet again, with significant help from his slightly mad corps commander Thomas Jonathan Jackson, Old Stonewall. With Confederate forces outnumbered almost two to one, the two devised a plan in which their forces would be split, Jackson taking his corps around the Union lines by a secret road to surprise Hooker's right flank, which lay completely unprotected by natural or military barriers. It was Jackson's smashing attack that caused the ensuing panic and rout of the Union army, sending them stumbling back through the woods.

A second story, more of a mystery really, was Hooker's decision-making during the battle. Initially marching his forces confidently southward with a nervous Lee in pursuit, Hooker seemed to lose his nerve as soon as the Union forces reached the densely forested area near the Chancellor's inn, and he slowed the pace of his march. At first contact with Confederate forces, Hooker actually backed up his lines and moved them into defensive positions, despite overwhelming numbers. Perhaps most puzzling of all was why Hooker left his right flank hanging in open country, all but inviting attack.

Tragically for the Confederate military, the third story involved the death of Stonewall Jackson. In his eagerness to follow up on the stunning initial success of his attack on the Union right flank, he and a small escort rode forward through the darkening woods to assess the wisdom of continuing to advance, and he was shot by his own troops. A ball went through his right hand, and he lost his left arm to amputation, but he seemed to be recovering from his wounds when pneumonia found him and carried him off a few days later. As he lay in a delirious fever near the end, Lee was quoted by some in his headquarters as saying that though Jackson had lost his left arm, Lee himself had lost his right.

For the men of the Union army, the outcome of the battle was sadly all too familiar. Yet another blustering commander had taken up the mantle of leadership with visions of glory and had come to grief at the hands of a wiser foe. And yet again the commander and the gray beards in the War Department engaged in a heated skirmish by telegraph, accusing and deflecting while the Army of the Potomac marched wearily north. Leaders in high command at times received censure and reassignment when battles were lost, but it was the men in the ranks who truly suffered.

Company D and its division remained encamped just east of the battleground for several days, keeping a wary eye on Lee's forces. When cavalry scouts reported clear signs of the main Confederate body moving south, the division decamped and marched north to join the rest of the army. On the way, they halted for a night near a field hospital to pick up such wounded as were still able to fight. Nathan was sent with a squad from the company to find three of its soldiers. By now Nathan was well used to the sensory assault of the hospital tent, but the men with him were new to it. One man stumbled outside and vomited, and the others were white-faced.

Nathan approached a nurse and asked after the men they were looking for. She consulted a chart and pointed toward the far end of the tent. Nathan thanked her and began walking in that direction when he heard someone call his name. He turned and saw a nurse he knew from Harewood walking toward him. Her name was Harriet, one of the kindest women Nathan had ever known.

She embraced him and then stepped back and held his hands. "Oh, Nathan. I am so glad to see you alive and well."

"You too, Harriet. How are things here?"

"The usual misery. Too many wounded, too few staff and supplies." She shrugged. "We do what we can."

Nathan looked about. "Any other familiar faces?"

A shadow crossed Harriet's face. "There were." "What do you mean?"

"A group of us came down with Nurse Barton. We . . ." She stopped and closed her eyes. "What is it, Harriet?"

"We set up a hospital tent not far from the inn." Harriet was crying now. "Maria was part of the group. Near the end of the battle, I was sent to meet a wagon train to pick up supplies, and when I came back—." She stopped again.

Nathan's blood went cold. "Please, tell me," he said softly.

"A shell had hit the tent and exploded. Everyone inside was killed."

Nathan looked at Harriet's face with unseeing eyes. His mouth opened and shut several times. He stood and breathed while the world moved around him. Eventually, he was aware of Harriet's hand on his arm. She was talking to him, but he was not hearing her. She hugged him tightly and moved off, wiping her eyes with her apron.

The other men of the squad found him, trailed by the wounded from their company. The corporal in charge of the detail looked at Nathan and his eyes narrowed in concern. He called Nathan's name, and slowly Nathan's eyes came up to meet his. The corporal ordered the men to guide on him, and they walked out of the tent into the sunlight.

Nathan remembered nothing of the march back to the camp. When the detail was dismissed, he walked aimlessly around the camp and then found his way to his shelter and sat outside it.

Joshua was sitting on a log mending socks. When he saw Nathan, he put down the sewing. "Nathan, what's wrong?"

He was empty. There was no thought in his brain to form into words, no air to make a sound to push out of his mouth. He sat like a stone.

Joshua stood up. "Nathan? Brother, what's the matter?"

Slowly and softly, Nathan breathed her name. "Maria."

"Maria? What about her? Is she all right? Where is she?"

Nathan summoned just enough strength to shake his head once.

"I don't know what that means." Joshua was now kneeling in front of Nathan, his face a mask of worry. "What happened to her?"

From a thousand miles away, Nathan heard himself say the word, "Dead."

Joshua sat back on his haunches and bowed his head. "No. Please, God, no." He leaned forward and took Nathan in his arms. Nathan made no effort to return the embrace, but Joshua did not let go. They sat in that position for a long time, saying nothing. Finally, Joshua released Nathan and sat beside him. There were no more words to say.

The next few days saw Nathan moving woodenly through the routines of camp. When he was on duty, he performed his tasks without speaking. When he was off duty, he walked into the woods and sat under a tree, staring at nothing. The chaplain came to speak with him, but Nathan brushed him off. Other than answering officers, when necessary, he only spoke with Joshua and very little at that. His heart was shattered; his soul more embittered by the moment.

Sunday came and the company was assembled for divine services. They sat in a small clearing, the warm sun of late spring on their uncovered heads. The chaplain led them in a few hymns and then began to speak, using as his text a passage from the second chapter of Ephesians. Nathan was awash in anger and tuned out the man's words for a time, settling instead on watching the birds flit through the trees. After a while he became bored and brought his focus back to the old preacher, who was coming to the conclusion of his sermon:

I have been speaking to you about God's amazing grace this morning. In a few minutes, I will be leading us in singing a beautiful old hymn that speaks to exactly that. Some of you may know the story of John Newton, who wrote this hymn almost one hundred years ago. John Newton was the captain of a slave ship and an investor in the slave trade in the mid-1700s.

During one voyage carrying human cargo from the shores of Africa, a great storm arose, and the young man feared for his life. He recounts in later writings that God met him in that storm and showed him the depths of his depravity, the absolute need for a Savior, and the astounding gift of grace that God was offering him.

From that time forward John Newton dedicated his life to sharing the good news of God's grace to all who would listen, and he was a staunch supporter of the abolitionist movement in England until his death.

How could such a man be considered worthy by God to become such a powerful instrument for His kingdom? Grace. Simply, grace. John Newton did nothing to deserve such a mighty, eternal gift. He was living far apart from God, destined for a life of misery and spiritual death. But the very definition of grace is "undeserved favor," and that is exactly what God bestowed on John Newton, through the sacrifice of Jesus Christ on Newton's behalf.

I bring your attention back to verse four of the second chapter of Ephesians, which begins, "But God." Gentlemen, I submit to you that these are two of the most powerful words in the entire Bible. They ring with this absolute truth: without God, we have no hope, and because of Him we have all hope. God extends the gift of grace to all whose hearts are ready to receive it.

Why does God do this? Because of His great love for us, and His wish for us to be free—free of fear, free of pride, free of envy, free of doubt, free of confusion, free of empty pursuits and self-striving, free of anger and despair and crushing grief.

As Paul writes to the church in Galatia in Gal. 5:1, the King James Version says we are to "stand fast therefore in the liberty wherewith Christ hath made us free." To put it more simply, the English Standard Version says, "For freedom Christ has set us free."

The chaplain continued but Nathan's mind was somewhere else. There was a distant memory like a wisp of smoke, something from the previous fall at Antietam. He had been preparing to leave for the orderly job in Washington, and somebody had given him something. Suddenly it came to him. Ezekiel handed him the slip of paper with the exact words the chaplain had just said. Nathan glanced up and the chaplain was looking right at him, smiling and raising his hands to lead the last hymn, "Amazing Grace." He closed his eyes and sang with gusto in a warbling baritone, oblivious to the half-hearted singing from the company.

After a closing prayer, the company was ordered to fall in and marched back to the camp. Sergeant Jeremiah assigned details, and the company was dismissed. Nathan and several others were assigned to gather firewood, and after this, he walked to his shelter and rummaged through his knapsack to find the paper. Eventually, he found it wrapped up in a small tin with his writing supplies. He took it out and looked at it, then put it back in the tin. They were just words on paper, nothing more.

For the next few weeks, the Army of the Potomac moved very little, staying near the Rappahannock River while General Hooker argued with the War Department about his next move. He wanted to drive toward Richmond again, but this caused the men in Washington concern, believing that such a move would leave the northern capital vulnerable to attack from an opponent who had proven his audacity more than once. And so, the volley of telegraphs continued, and the men of the Army of the Potomac sat in their camps, waiting for their military leaders to come up with the next plan. The men of Company D bided their time with the rest, seeking shade where they could as the heat of summer encroached.

If the War Department had known what Lee was up to, their concern would have quickly escalated to alarm. While Lee's army rested and recuperated from the recent battle, the wheels in the old man's mind were turning. He saw in Hooker's hesitant leadership and the current disposition of the northern army an opportunity to potentially accomplish several important goals for the Confederate military cause. He did much of his thinking in the early morning hours when little was stirring in camp. At these times he often strolled out to the corral where his horse Traveller was kept. He would pat the animal's graceful neck and ruminate while his faithful companion looked on with large brown eyes.

After days of thought, Lee had what he felt was a clear and compelling plan. He sent a telegraph to Jefferson Davis in Richmond, asking for a meeting. Wary of spies in the Confederate capital, Davis suggested meeting on a boat out on the James River. Lee agreed, and a date and time were set.

It was a small group that gathered on the Richmond docks on a warm and hazy June morning. Other than a squad of protective cavalry, which waited on the shore, Lee brought only his most trusted aide, the efficient and energetic Walter Taylor. Jefferson was accompanied by his vice president, Alexander Stephens. The small and painfully thin Georgian was as usual bundled up in an oversized coat and a scarf, always leery of a sudden draft or chill. The four men boarded the vessel and were soon headed away from shore.

They sat at a table in a small dining room. Drinks were offered and Lee declined with his usual gracious Virginia manners. Davis took a small sip of whiskey and began.

"Well, General. Again, I wish to congratulate you on your splendid victory at Chancellorsville."

Lee bowed slightly. "You are too kind, Mr. President. But I must insist that this victory was not mine alone. I had enormous help from aides such as Mr. Taylor here, as well as my field commanders. And as you well know, Mr. President, battles are won by soldiers rather than generals, and the men fought magnificently." He grew quiet and looked down at the table.

Guessing at Lee's mood, Davis said, "Sad business about Jackson. He will be sorely missed."

"Yes, I feel it keenly." Lee sighed and the room lapsed again into silence, which was eventually broken by a fit of coughing from Stephens, who attempted to muffle it with an enormous handkerchief.

Davis waited patiently for quiet and then spoke. "General, you mentioned in your recent telegram that you have come up with a strategy that involves the Army of Northern Virginia striking north. I am most eager to hear details."

Lee motioned to Taylor who handed him a leather case from which Lee drew out a small sheaf of papers and slid them across the table to Davis. "Mr. President, these are maps and written plans of my proposal, which you may keep and read through at your convenience, for reference. I wish to lay out my proposal to you verbally, sir, if that is acceptable to you."

"Yes, General, that is acceptable. And I am grateful for these notes, being a man who, as you know, appreciates detail. I will be sure to share this information with the War Department. You may proceed."

Lee nodded. He looked down for a moment to finalize his thoughts, picked a piece of lint off his immaculate uniform, and began.

His plan was tactically rather simple, with the army marching north by corps, over seventy thousand men, up through Maryland and into Pennsylvania, using the Blue Ridge Mountains as a natural screen and protection for their right flank. J. E. B. Stuart, Lee's dandily dressed and eminently capable cavalry commander, would provide further screening for the main body and detailed information regarding Federal troop movements.

The plan was strategically driven by three main objectives: to take the initiative away from Hooker in this next phase of the chess game, to force the Union army into a disadvantaged fight to protect their capital, and to resupply and feed the Confederate army from the country that had not yet been ravaged by war.

Davis listened attentively as Lee spoke, occasionally asking a clarifying question. Stephens, a nervous man by disposition, fidgeted almost constantly, but his keen mind missed nothing. By the time Lee finished, the boat had turned back downriver and was nearing the docks. Once the boat was tied up, the four men disembarked and shook hands all around. Davis assured Lee that he would gather his war council posthaste to discuss Lee's proposal and send their answer as soon as practicable. Lee bowed graciously. He and Taylor mounted their horses and rode off with the cavalry escort. Davis watched them go, thanking God for the hundredth time for blessing the Confederacy with such a brilliant military mind.

On the Union side, there was only more waiting. Under the guise of allowing the army to rest and refit after the mauling received at Chancellorsville, Hooker dithered with his commanders and complained about interference from Washington. His generals and aides-de-camp offered new strategies, and he dismissed them. They suggested that he send out cavalry to learn of Lee's intentions, and he did not. The wind seemed to have gone from his sails. Some of the older officers on his staff had seen this in his predecessors and shook their heads. What the Army of the Potomac needed now was a man of foresight, confidence, and action, and Joseph Hooker exuded none of these at the moment.

In the Company D encampment, the mood was grim and despondent, closely matching that of the rest of the army. Men were edgy and irritable, fights and desertions increased again, and officers tightened the reins, though this time with a measure of compassion, sharing much the same mood as the men they commanded.

Joshua watched his brother with growing concern. Never had Nathan seemed so bitter and closed off. He moved as though driven by machinery. The only emotion that seemed left in him was seething anger. Thrice in a week, Joshua had had to step between his brother and another soldier before an argument came to blows. Joshua soon gave up trying to talk with Nathan about anything other than daily camp details. He never mentioned Maria.

He obsessively cleaned his musket, making sure that it was in perfect working order. Some of the sergeants in the company complimented him on the care of his weapon for a time, but gradually they began to share Joshua's concern, and they watched Nathan quietly. He seemed to be waiting only for the next battle, the next opportunity to inflict death.

In early June Lee received the answer he was hoping for in a telegram from Davis. He had held his forces in readiness to march for some days in hopeful anticipation, and now he gave orders to start the army moving. The Army of Northern Virginia quietly slipped away from the Union lines and headed north.

It was almost two weeks later that Hooker finally listened to nervous cavalry reports of Lee's movements and got his force of over one hundred thousand underway, to keep pace with the Gray Fox. All along the march, Hooker received telegram after telegram from the War Department, nagging him to keep between the Confederates and halt their northward advance. It became a sort of game for Hooker's aides to watch the general stomp around outside his tent while ripping up the latest missive from Washington.

Slowly, the two armies wound their way through northern Virginia and then Maryland. Lee and his men more often than not were met with cheers and offers of food by the Marylanders as they marched through the small towns and hamlets. The state had been of divided loyalties since before the start of the war, and its citizens seemed no closer now to a united mind. It was quite common to see flags hung out of windows, displaying the stars and bars of the St. Andrew's cross.

The Union army experienced a more mixed reception. As they proceeded north, some townspeople were glad to see the men in blue, ready to protect their farms and homes from the rebel invaders. Others were indifferent, believing that this war was not their concern. Still, others were outright hostile, shouting from their porches for the army to keep marching along and leave their state. Officers kept a close eye on the men in ranks and the citizenry, some remembering the riots that had occurred in this state two years ago when Union forces had first marched south.

As the Confederates neared the Pennsylvania border, Hooker sent word to commanders of nearby garrisons to send additional troops to him. General in Chief Henry Halleck, who had never liked Hooker, promptly rescinded his orders, and in a fit of temper, Hooker offered the War Department his resignation. Lincoln heard out his cabinet's opinions and weighed options in his mind. He realized that changing commanders just before what could be a major battle was a risky move. He also believed that on the whole Hooker had proven to be an ineffective commander, at least when tested in battle. In the end, Lincoln decided to accept Hooker's resignation and promote George Meade to the head of the Army of the Potomac. Meade was currently commanding a corps. An engineer by profession, he had served with distinction in the Mexican American War and called Pennsylvania his home. He moved slowly and had a quick temper, earning him the nickname "Old Snapping Turtle." And so, the Union forces continued their pursuit of Lee under yet another leader.

Company D was encamped in an open field after a hot and dusty march. The men were sitting around small fires eating supper. Conversations centered mainly around the change in command. Hooker had been popular among the rank and file for his provision of practical care for them, but they had experienced the devastating consequences of his faulty battle command. Meade was largely an unknown quantity. Those who had energy entered into a lively debate.

Nathan was indifferent to this topic. He soon tired of the talk and went to his shelter. A few minutes after he had lain down, he heard Joshua's familiar steps approaching. They stopped just outside the shelter. "Nathan?"

Something in Joshua's voice made Nathan sit up and look outside. His brother was silhouetted in the evening light, a letter in his hand. His face was still and pale. Nathan stood up and put a hand on his shoulder. "Joshua, what is it?"

"The mail . . ." Joshua stopped and took a breath. "The mail finally caught up to us. We got this from Rachael." He stopped again.

"What? What does it say?" Nathan had rarely seen his brother this shaken, and it unnerved him.

"Father is dead." Joshua's mouth hardly moved. "He had a massive stroke about a week ago and died in the night. The church had a service for him."

A lump began to form in Nathan's throat. He swallowed and looked past Joshua at the sun beginning its descent. He had no words.

"We can ask Captain Shields about going home—" He heard himself say, "They won't let us go. Not now."

The letter fluttered to the ground and Joshua began to cry softly. Nathan stepped forward and embraced him, feeling his brother's body shudder as the sadness poured out of him. His own grief was inaccessible just now, and so he held Joshua close. The thought struck him that they were orphans now. Under that was only a deep, smoldering anger—toward the enemy that had taken so much from him, and a distant and uncaring God who had done nothing to stop it.

The main part of this enemy was some miles to the east, also encamped for the night. Two corps had marched ahead across the border into Pennsylvania toward Cashtown, having heard that there were badly needed shoes and other supplies to be had in that area. Lee was nervous about his army being strung out on the march, especially as he had not heard from Stuart in some days. The gallant cavalry commander had ridden away from the main body to do some raiding, leaving Lee to only guess at Union strength and positions, and the geography of the country in which they now found themselves.

As the last day of June approached, Lee, desperate for information, turned to his faithful lieutenant James Longstreet for help. The gloomy corps commander had made acquaintances with an actor of little fame named Harrison, who had made himself a career of spying for the Confederates. The diminutive and clever man now delivered critical information to Longstreet that the Army of the Potomac was very close and in great numbers. Longstreet delivered this news to Lee personally. The great commander looked skeptically at Longstreet as he spoke between puffs on a cigar. In the end, Lee chose to act on the intelligence just received. He and Longstreet studied a map of the area. Lee was looking for a place to concentrate his forces quickly, and the town of Gettysburg suited his purpose. Noting that several roads led directly to the town itself, he quickly sent out riders to his corps commanders to the north, urging them to turn and march south with all possible speed toward the sleepy little place known mostly for its Lutheran seminary.

To the west, Meade fretted and grumped at his aides as he tried to discern Lee's intentions. Fortunately, his cavalry commander, John Buford, was close at hand. The hard-bitten Kentuckian had served with distinction in the Mexican War and through the first two years of this conflict. Meade had heard of the general's forthright and effective leadership from others, and he was about to find out for himself. He sent Buford and his troopers ahead of the main body to scout the area around Gettysburg and get a fix on Lee.

The Union cavalry reached the town on the last day of June, and Buford immediately saw good high ground just to the north and west. His scouts had found the approaching Confederates and noted their dispositions, Buford had his troopers dismount and deployed them. He set up headquarters at the seminary and sent a message to John Reynolds, commander of the corps whose infantry was closest. Buford quickly described his situation and urged Reynolds to come up as quickly as possible, believing that a major engagement was imminent. Satisfied that he had done all he could for the day, he curled up in a blanket under a tree in the seminary yard and waited for sleep.

He did not get much as it turned out. His mind continued working for much of the night about the coming battle, which he could see clearly in his imagination. Before dawn, an aide woke him to say that Confederate infantry was only a few miles away. Buford roused himself and put on his old, battered campaign hat. He quickly drank a cup of coffee and put a piece of fried salt pork in his haversack, knowing from experience that he would think more clearly if he had something in his stomach. With a deep sigh, he settled himself in the saddle and rode out to review the positions of his men.

The day had dawned warm and clear. As Buford approached his forward positions, the sun was beginning to burn off the dew on the grass, causing a mist to rise from the ground. Buford sat in the saddle joined by his brigade commanders, all looking into the near distance through field glasses. As they sighted down the nearest road, they began to see a low cloud of dust rising above the mist. Buford gave quick orders for the artillery to prepare to fire, and his troopers hunkered down with their carbines behind stone and split rail fences.

In a surprisingly short time, a Confederate infantry brigade came over a low rise and began to file into the fields in front of the Union positions. Union artillery began a barrage on the Confederate flanks, soon joined by the troopers with small arms fire. The Confederates seemed at first surprised and disorganized by the strength of the Union presence in front of them, but commanders quickly got their men online and returned fire. Nevertheless, the initial Confederate assault was blunted by the fierce and accurate fire of the Union cavalry, and soon there was a lull in the fighting. Buford nodded to himself in grim satisfaction and took a bite of the salt pork, calculating his next moves as he watched more Confederate infantry come up the road to add weight to the next attack.

As the morning wore on, it became apparent that the Confederate advance was too powerful to hold back much longer. Buford sent an urgent message to Reynolds, asking when he might get on the field. He climbed into the seminary cupola and watched as the Union troopers were pushed steadily back toward the town. Then an aide appeared at his side with news that two additional Confederate corps were bearing down on them from the north and west. Buford anxiously turned his field glasses to the south and spied a small group of horsemen riding toward the seminary, bearing the flag of the 1st Corps. He breathed a quick prayer of thanks and waited until Reynolds himself was within hailing distance. The corps commander calmly reined in and looked up. "How goes it, John?"

Buford wiped his brow on a sleeve. "It's a tough business, sir. We're tangled with at least one corps now, with two more on the way from the north."

"Can you hold them a bit longer?"

"I reckon so."

"Very good. I will tell my commanders to bring their men up with all possible speed. They are not far behind me, actually. The Black Hats will most definitely be heard from today."

Buford nodded. "We'll keep the rebels tied up in the meantime."

Reynolds gave him a confident wave and rode back the way he had come, with his aides in tow. Buford watched him go for a bit, then turned back to the battle in front of him.

Even with the 1st Corps coming online beside the Union troopers and another infantry corps on the way, the weight of the Confederate attack began to break the Union lines as the day went on. There was savage fighting in a railroad cut, and Reynolds himself was felled by a sniper's bullet. Soon the Union troops were pushed back through the town and ended up taking defensive positions to the south. Their right flank surrounded a low hill in a hook, then extended south along a ridge close to a cemetery, and the left was anchored on a small round hill overlooked by a larger hill.

Both sides were exhausted and bloodied by day's end, but Lee had cause to celebrate as his troops bedded down for the night. He held the town and good ground to the north and west of the Union positions. Even though a golden opportunity had been missed by one of his corps commanders to take the high ground on the Union right flank, Lee still felt that he had the advantage so far in this fight. Meade was back on his heels, and Lee intended to hit him hard the next day.

Company D was encamped along with its regiment in a small grove of trees less than ten miles from Gettysburg. They had marched long and hard that day in the heat, urged on by their commanders, and they were exhausted. Several men had gone down with heat stroke.

When they were finally given the order to halt, it was nearly dark. They could hear the low rumble of artillery in the distance, but most of them didn't care—they wanted food and sleep. Tomorrow would bring its own issues.

Nathan and Joshua had finished eating and were sitting around a small fire with several others from the company. There was little talk as most of their energy had been used up on the march. Before long most had gone off to their shelters, leaving only the two brothers. There was silence between them for a time. Then Joshua spoke.

"I miss Father."

Nathan did not reply.

"Do you not miss him, brother?" Still, Nathan was silent.

Joshua leaned forward. "Surely you have some feelings about this! Where is your heart?" "I have known a lot of death recently, Joshua. My heart is used to it by now."

"I know that you grieve Maria's death, Nathan. But don't let that overshadow your love for Father."

Nathan spoke quietly. "My love for them is different, and neither overshadows the other. I simply choose to not live in grief."

"So, you choose to live in anger, then." Joshua's voice had a bitter edge.

"What is it to you?"

"Because I care for your soul!"

"What does my soul have to do with this?"

"Everything!"

Nathan stomped a foot on the ground. "Don't bring God into this! Do not! I have had my fill of talk about a loving and merciful being who cares for His creation!"

Joshua held a hand out toward his brother. "Nathan, please. Do you really hold God responsible for all those we have lost?"

"Yes, I do."

"What good will it do to be angry with Him?"

Nathan looked up at his brother, his eyes glittering in the firelight. "It is the only thing keeping me going."

"But—."

"No," Nathan spoke slowly, emphasizing his words with a pointing finger. "This anger is mine. And no one, including God, can take it from me."

Joshua had no reply to this, and silence returned. The fire crackled. An owl hooted in a nearby tree. Finally, Joshua sighed and said, "I love you, brother."

"I love you, too."

"I pray that God will soften your heart."

"Do as you will."

Joshua stood and stretched. "Come on, you stubborn ass. Let's get some sleep. I have a feeling we're going to need it."

Nathan smiled faintly and followed his brother back to their shelter.

On the ridge south of the seminary was a small house in which Lee had set up his headquarters. He had talked with his field commanders and had studied hastily sketched maps of the current Union and Confederate positions. He sat in a rocking chair by a small hearth fire, thinking through the details of his assault plan for the following day. He had just finished a short and intense interview with J. E. B. Stuart. The young cavalry commander had sauntered into headquarters earlier that evening, beaming with pride at the results of his raiding. He had left a much-humbled man, having felt the anger and disappointment of his beloved leader for leaving the army blind at a critical point.

The exchange had left Lee drained. He was not normally given to displays of temper as he felt it was unbecoming for an officer. However, he believed he needed to make it very clear to Stuart what was expected of him going forward, and so he had let loose some fire in the hopes of further refining an already strong commander. But this, along with the heat and other cares of the day, took what energy he had left. An ongoing heart condition further taxed him this night.

He began to nod off and was gently awakened by Walter Taylor, who tucked a blanket around him and asked if there was anything else the general required."

"Thank you, no, Mr. Taylor. You have been quite enough help today. You should get some rest."

"I can do what is needed, sir. Just say the word."

Lee gave him a kindly dismissive gesture. "Walter, you may retire. God be with you."

Taylor gave him a crisp salute. "And with you, sir." With that, he made his way to a small room in the back of the house.

Lee stayed up a bit longer, staring into the fire. His last waking thoughts, after a short time of prayer, were of his wife and his home in Virginia.

The day began gray and humid. Lee dressed by candlelight and sent for Longstreet. He walked to the corral where Traveller was kept, savoring the quiet of the morning. Longstreet arrived shortly looking rumpled and tired, yet managed a crisp salute. Lee got straight to the point, outlining his battle plan for the day. Believing that Union forces were shaken from the events of yesterday, he thought that strong, coordinated attacks all along their lines would shake them loose from their positions and send them fleeing east in disarray, allowing his army to pursue at their leisure and threaten Washington. He finished speaking and saw the hesitation on Longstreet's face.

"What are you thinking, General?"

The corps commander was quiet for a moment, then spoke slowly and carefully. "Sir, the Federal positions seem quite strong on both flanks, particularly on the rocky heights to the south. Would it not be to our advantage to move around to the right of that position? That way the Federals would be forced to abandon their lines to keep between us and Washington, and we could fight them on the ground of our choosing."

Lee shook his head. "We prevailed yesterday, and morale is high. To disengage from the enemy now would be dangerous and appear weak. No, General. The enemy is here, and we must fight him here."

"I just—."

"General Longstreet, the plan will proceed as I have explained it. You have good officers under you, the men are strong and ready to fight, and I believe that we will prevail again this day. Now look to your corps, General."

Longstreet straightened and saluted. "Yes, sir." He signaled for his horse and rode off to the south, a sense of foreboding in his chest.

He went in search of John Bell Hood, one of his most trusted division commanders. The hard-fighting Kentuckian was currently in position with his forces directly across from the Union left flank. Longstreet found him talking with some of his aides. He dismounted and motioned Hood aside. Hood saluted him and they walked away from the camp. Hood could sense disquiet in his friend.

"What's on your mind, Pete?"

Longstreet stopped and lit a cigar. "I talked with General Lee this morning. His orders are for coordinated attacks along the whole Union line today as soon as practicable, starting with their left flank. I want you to lead the attack on this flank with your division."

Hood turned and looked at the rocky heights, then back at Longstreet. "Pete, have you taken a good look at these positions? We have no cover, the Federals are dug in tight, and the ground up there is terrible."

Longstreet took a puff on his cigar and said nothing.

"It would make a whole lot more sense to move around to the right. Make them come to us."

"I mentioned that to General Lee, and he is firm on his plan."

"Pete, if I send my division up those rocks, I'm going to lose a lot of good men today."

Longstreet threw his cigar to the ground in frustration. "Just get your troops ready to attack as soon as you can, General."

Hood made as if to speak and then drew himself up and saluted. "Yes, General. But I do this under protest." He turned and barked at one of his aides. Longstreet mounted his horse and turned to the north. He wondered grimly if he would ever see his friend again.

The attacks were delayed and uncoordinated, as it took longer than usual to deploy troops, and communication between units was haphazard. By the time the Confederates moved forward, the skies had mostly cleared, and a hazy sun brought the heat down on the battlefield. The battle on the Union right flank was a chaotic and bloody affair from the beginning, and before long the ground was carpeted with dead and wounded.

If possible, the fight on the other flank was worse. Hood began to move his men up the hills and initially gained some ground, but as he had predicted, the terrain was nearly impossible to traverse, and his momentum stalled. There was a brief lull in the fighting while Hood reorganized his troops for another assault.

On the ground in front of the rocky heights, Union general Dan Sickles waited with his corps. A general more through political avenues than military experience, he was most notable for having shot his wife's lover in the streets of New York City several years earlier. This day he stood impatiently as the sounds of battle raged around him. He called for field glasses from an aide and looked out in front of his position. He spied a small knoll in an orchard of peach trees and decided to move his entire corps forward to the higher ground. What ensued over the next several hours was nothing less than carnage. Sickles' corps suffered horrific casualties as it was savaged by Confederate troops on three sides.

Not only was the move harmful to Sickles' corps, but it also uncovered the rocky heights and breathed new life into Hood's assault. He ordered seven separate attacks up the stony ground, and only the bravery and sheer grit of the Union troops there saved the Union left flank that day. Above all stood the leadership of Joshua Lawrence Chamberlain, a college professor from Maine, who in desperation ordered what was left of his regiment to a bayonet charge down the slope, stunning the exhausted Confederates and effectively ending the flank assault.

Several miles to the south, Company D and its division were being hurried forward. They had been wakened early and told to fill their cartridge boxes and canteens but otherwise travel light. The heat of the day kept the ranks mostly quiet as they marched, that and the sounds of a significant battle to their front. They moved quickly at the route step, not stopping for food or rest or even when men began to succumb to the heat. They passed by fields of wheat and corn and the occasional farmhouse, but there were no people to be seen.

Eventually, the troops topped a low rise and could see the faint outlines of a town in the distance. Smoke and haze obscured all but a few details. The sounds of battle suddenly grew louder. Joshua nudged Nathan and pointed excitedly. "Do you see that white cupola just to the left at the far end of the town?"

Nathan had been lost in his own thoughts. He now looked where Joshua was pointing but could not see the landmark his brother referred to. "I don't."

"Well, I do. That's the dear old seminary, brother. I wasn't sure I'd ever see it again."

Nathan had nothing further to say on the matter and lapsed back into silence. The man in front of him staggered and caught himself, then fell to the ground and lay still. Nathan stumbled over him but managed to keep his balance. A sergeant pulled the man to the side of the road and barked to the men to keep moving.

It was mid-afternoon when the division passed two hills on their left. Dense smoke rose through the trees near the crown of the hill to the north, and the muffled tearing of musket fire reached their ears. A rider approached the division staff at the head of the column, and Nathan could see him shouting and pointing ahead and to the left. He turned his horse and rode just to the front, serving as a guide.

With the two hills behind them, the column marched by the left flank off the main road onto a lesser trail. They passed an immense artillery park, and Nathan thought of Billy. He scanned the park for the familiar giant silhouette, but all was flurry and confusion. Now they marched through wagon trains, with cavalry pickets roaming the perimeter on high alert. Reserve infantry units sat or stood restlessly. Wounded and dead lay scattered on the ground. Occasionally, a shell whistled through the air and landed close by, throwing up dirt and sending men and horses scrambling for safety. The bitter smell of gunpowder was thick in the air.

The column was halted, and orders went through the ranks to drink. The weary men gratefully lowered their musket butts to the ground and uncorked their canteens. Nathan took out a handkerchief, a gift from Rachael, and wetted it. He patted the back of his neck and wiped his face, feeling a small measure of relief. A headache had been nagging him all day, and the heat and dust of the march had made it worse. Up ahead he could see the division staff talking with two more riders. He knew from experience that when the conversation concluded, they would most likely be called to attention in short order. With the sun beginning its downward slope and, in his eyes, he brought up a hand to shade them and watched until he saw the riders salute and ride off. He nudged Joshua, and they prepared for the march. In less than a minute Captain Shields unsheathed his sword and called the company to attention, and they stepped off.

On the ridge behind the seminary, Lee sat astride Traveller. All day he had been receiving news from riders and aides as to the disposition of the battle. He now knew that both flank attacks had been stopped. He also knew that Sickles had created an enormous gap in the Union lines by moving his corps forward. He had hoped that Richard Anderson's corps would have attacked sooner toward the center of the Union line, thus fully exploiting Sickles' tragic blunder, but it couldn't be helped now.

As he pondered these things, Walter Taylor rode up and saluted. "General Lee, I am told that Anderson's corps is now in position to advance."

"Mr. Taylor, tell General Anderson to attack at once."

"Yes, sir." Taylor saluted quickly and galloped off.

Lee nodded to himself. If the Union troops to his right were as decimated as he had been told, Anderson might yet achieve a significant breakthrough before the sun set. "It is in God's hands now," he murmured.

Anderson received the order and sent a division forward immediately. One of the first brigades to march down the gentle slope toward the Union center was made up largely of men from Mississippi and Alabama. These men had served long and hard in the war and were prepared for a hard fight. As they passed through a line of trees and approached a dry creek bed, they were surprised to find almost no Union troops facing them. Their officers looked at one another in disbelief, shrugged their shoulders, and urged their men forward.

Company D's division marched directly into the setting sun. Shot and shell began to land on either side of the column, and then on the column itself as Confederate artillery adjusted their fire. Company D and its brigade were marched off to the right, heading for a downward slope. Nathan looked back toward the rest of the division and saw a drummer boy shot through the eye. Other men began to fall as bullets came at them from the opposite slope.

Nathan looked ahead and saw a huge open space going down toward a dry creek bed. One small regiment of Union troops, no more than three hundred men by his estimate, stood in that space near an artillery battery. Company D's brigade was halted and arranged in a column of companies, all on battlefront, Company D in the second position.

Nathan watched an officer ride in from the right toward the regiment near the creek bed. He reined in and shouted toward the commanding officer, then pointed toward the opposite slope. The officer on the ground saluted and gave an order, and the regiment began fixing bayonets.

Nathan looked across from them and his jaw dropped. Confederate troops at least five times the number of the Union regiment were coming down the slope. It was an impossible thing.

With his heart in his throat, Nathan watched the regiment shift their muskets to Charge Bayonet and step off. A slight breeze came up and unfurled the regimental flag.

Now Company D was ordered to load muskets and fix bayonets. Nathan finished quickly and looked to his left. He caught Joshua's eye and Joshua flashed him a fierce grin.

He looked ahead again and saw the troops running across the creek bed with bayonets leveled. It looked like half or more were down.

Captain Shields turned and faced the two ranks. "Company D! Order, arms!"

A shell landed just at the left end of the line, throwing several men into the air. A leg cartwheeled forward and narrowly missed the captain.

"Front rank! Three paces forward!"

Slap. The man on Nathan's right grunted and slumped against him before falling to the ground. Nathan reached up and felt something warm and wet on his face.

"Charge, bayonet!"

The captain turned on his heel until he was facing front. He drew his sword and pointed it forward. "At the double quick! Forward, march!"

Time slowed to a crawl. The sound was distorted as if coming down a long tunnel. Jogging forward.

The wind rushed past his ears.

Running to the neighbor's house, Mother bleeding at the cabin. The setting sun filtered through the trees.

Sitting with Rachael on the porch.

Two men in front of him bump into each other and fall. Shouting all around him.

The docks at Charleston, the angry crowd. Stepping over dead and dying men.

A regimental flag fluttering. Minnesota. *L'etoile du Nord*. What does that mean?

Looking to the left. Joshua with his head back, mouth open. Slap. Slap. Surprise on his face. A shout from his own throat.

An explosion. Joshua was thrown into the air like a rag doll. Like one of Rachael's childhood dolls. He lands and lies still.

Boiling up in him, from way down deep. Growing, rising. A volcano churning, hot and acid in his mouth. Rage.

Looking forward. An angry bee zipped past his head. A burning sensation on his neck. Tears stung his eyes.

Stumbling through weeds at the edge of the creek bed. Vaulting to the other side. More bodies. A man clutching at his leg.

Ahead are blurry figures, brown and blue and grey. Beards and battered hats. The smells of sweat and gunpowder.

In front of him was a small man in a red checkered shirt.

Picnics on the church lawn.

His mouth opened with a savage roar, leveling his bayonet at the checkered shirt.

The jolt as the blade strikes home. The man's eyes flew wide. His mouth a perfect circle as air is driven from him, a high-pitched "Huh!"

A brilliant white light. Nothing.

7

A LOW SOUND, FAINT and far away. Moaning. Muffled popping sounds. Boots crunching on dry grass. Shouts in front and behind. The feel of something slightly rough on his cheek. The smell of dirt.

And singing. Someone singing softly, breathlessly. He knew it. A hymn. "Amazing Grace."

He realized he was lying on something that was not the ground. He still held tightly to his musket. There was an immense pain at the back of his head.

He tried to open his eyes. Blackness.

His left arm was pinned underneath him. He opened his right hand and moved that arm. The singing stopped, and he heard a grunt. He froze. After a minute he tried to move his right arm again.

Another grunt.

"Hello?"

A couple of ragged breaths, then a quiet voice. "Hello yourself, Yank." A deep Southern drawl. Nathan raised his head in alarm. "Who are you?"

"I am . . . a corporal . . . in the Confederate Army." He couldn't seem to say more than a few words at a time.

"Can you move?"

"Not especially. You are . . . lying on top of me."

"Hang on. I'll try to move." Strangely embarrassed, Nathan began to roll to one side.

A cough of agony. "Hold up there, Yank. It seems . . . that your bayonet . . . is in my chest."

"What?" And then the pictures returned, the ghastly ending before all went to nothingness. "Oh." Silence. "I don't know what to do." A realization. "I can't see."

"Not surprised. My pard . . . bashed your head . . . pretty good . . . with his musket."

Other than distant musket fire and the cries of the wounded nearby, all around seemed strangely quiet. "Is it over?"

"Guess so. At least for now."

Something was missing. It wasn't just the absence of battle - something inside him was different. The fire was gone. A strange emptiness in his soul. He began to think. "You need to get to a hospital." His head throbbed a reminder to him. "But I don't know how to do that."

"How close . . . are yours?"

He thought a moment. "Just over the ridge behind us."

A different voice near him murmured deliriously about Mary and the children.

The stranger spoke. "I got . . . an idea of sorts." A pause. "How about . . . you carry me . . . ... on your back . . . and I tell you . . . where to go."

For some incredible reason, he was not afraid of his sight being gone. The emptiness in him was calming. More incredible still, the man's idea made sense. "All right."

"Step one: get off me." The man sounded like he was instructing someone on how to build a wagon. "Gentle."

Slowly and with great care, Nathan rolled to his right and got both hands planted on the ground. Then he pushed himself up and straightened his legs. He inched himself backward until he was kneeling on the ground. He did not feel any other injuries. The man did not make a sound as Nathan moved.

" Next, take the bayonet out of me."

Nathan shuddered, remembering the grimness of bayonet drill: Thrust, develop, recover. Still, he allowed the man to verbally guide him to take hold of the musket and gently pull it out. He feared that it would be stuck, and he would have to twist the musket in the process, but it was not so. This time, the man gave a painful sigh. Nathan laid the musket on the ground and stood uncertainly.

"Now, get on your hands and knees next to me."

Nathan did so. He heard the man moan and move next to him. Then hands grabbed at his sack coat. A leg was swung over him and slowly, he felt the man's weight shift onto his back. Immediately, he felt warmth and wetness there, sweat and blood mingled together.

Now came the difficult part. Nathan gathered his legs under him and used his arms to steady himself. Then with some effort, he straightened. He was surprised at the lightness of the man. He felt a chin rest on his left shoulder. The man's breath smelled of apples.

"You doin' all right, Yank?"

He nodded.

"Over the ridge, you say?" Nathan nodded again.

"Well, step off when you're ready. I'll tell you where to put your feet."

Nathan took a deep breath and began to walk. The man's voice murmured in his ear, alerting him as needed to avoid obstacles on the ground, of which there were a great many at first. In this way, the unlikely pair made slow but steady progress.

Eventually, the obstacles became fewer, and the man began to hum very softly. Then he added words: "Amazing Grace! How sweet the sound, that saved a wretch like me . . ."

The emptiness in Nathan began to fill, as though with water.

"I once was lost, but now I'm found; was blind but now I see . . ."

He could taste it in the back of his throat, a great reservoir of sorrow. His eyes began to water. Walking, walking. The weight on his back, the warmth, the man's whiskers scratching his cheek.

"Twas grace that taught my heart to fear, and grace my fears relieved..."

He was crying now, tears coursing down his face. He murmured, "I'm sorry."

The man stopped singing. "You say something, Yank?"

He could hardly speak. A dam was bursting inside him, pouring out the misery of his years. "I'm . . . sorry."

"I forgive you." It was said so quietly that Nathan's ears could barely pick it up, and yet it seared through his brain like a lightning strike. He let out a sob.

"I forgive you." Just a whisper this time. He howled as bitterness and sorrow came out of him in a torrent. His mind could not fathom what he was hearing. His soul ached for it.

"I forgive you." Little more than a breath. Nathan staggered and caught himself. A poison was being leached out of him, a new energy taking its place.

He heard someone call to him. There was a hand on his arm, then other voices, hands gently taking the man off his back. He was guided to a tent, unmistakably a hospital given the smells and sounds that came from it. An orderly helped him to sit on a cot and told him that a surgeon would check him presently. He took off his sack coat and wiped his face with it. The orderly came back and gently washed his neck and put a bandage on it.

Time passed. Nathan strained to hear battle sounds, but there were none to speak of—only an occasional cannon or musket discharge. Even the hospital tent was unusually quiet. He turned his thoughts inward. For some reason he could not understand, he was not concerned about his sight. He was intrigued by a peace that lay gently on him. He wanted to know how and why it had come to him. Some intimate exchange had occurred between him and the man who had ridden on his back, a glorious release in the most unlikely of circumstances. He could make no sense of it.

A surgeon with a deep voice sat down beside him. He asked Nathan a few questions and probed the back of his head with delicate fingers. He sighed the very sound a portent of bad news. "Son, given the place and extent of the injury to your head, it is very likely that you will never see again." Nathan felt a warm hand on his shoulder. "I pray to God that I'm wrong."

"Doctor, that may be more in my department." The thick Swedish accent brought fresh tears to Nathan's eyes. "Thank you for your care of this young man. I am his company chaplain, and he and I need to have some words."

The cot gave a creak as the surgeon stood. "Very good, Chaplain. I will carry on with my rounds."

There were the sounds of a chair being dragged toward the cot and someone sitting, and then warm hands rested on Nathan's own. "So, my boy, how are you faring?"

"You heard the surgeon?"

"I did."

Nathan was quiet for a moment. "Chaplain, why am I not more afraid?"

"Tell me what happened before you were brought here."

For the next several minutes Nathan poured out his heart to the old Swede—every sight and thought and feeling he could remember, starting with the charge and ending with him sitting on the cot in a state of calm he had never known before. Finally, he ran out of words and fell silent.

"What did the man's words mean to you?"

"I don't know."

"Think harder."

I forgive you. "I've never heard anyone say those words to me."

"Are you sure?"

Nathan thought back over the whole of his life, from as far back as he could remember. "Yes, sir."

"Seems to me you are forgetting someone." "No one I can recall, sir."

"Someone who has always been with you, Nathan."

A light began to dawn in his mind. Somewhere in the teachings of his father, the words from a book Nathan had long ago stopped reading, the kindnesses of people familiar and strange, there had been a message.

"I can see it in your face, Nathan. You are beginning to understand. It is God who has told you that He has forgiven you and that He is watching over you. He is pouring out His grace on you—every day in a thousand different ways. Perhaps, just perhaps, even the man you carried here was a messenger from Him." There was a smile in the old man's voice.

Nathan's heart began to awaken, to rise up. And then it fell. "Sir, the things I've done in my life, today… I don't deserve forgiveness."

He was startled by the chaplain clapping his hands. "Yes! Think about the words of that hymn the man was singing."

"Amazing Grace."

"Yes, Nathan. Grace is undeserved favor. It is amazing because there is nothing we can do to earn it. God gives it to us for free, because He loves us. We were wretches, you and I, and He saved us."

"But how can it be that simple?"

The chaplain laughed heartily. "Did I say anything about simple? Men have devoted their entire lives to studying this very concept, and they still don't have a firm grasp on it."

"What hope do I have then, sir?"

The old man leaned forward. "Talk to Him Nathan. Talk to him every day, all the time. Read His Word. Find other believers and talk to them. Let God teach you more and more about His grace, His mercy, and His forgiveness. You will never be the same."

They talked on into the night. To the north of the hospital tent, a low rumble started becoming sharper and more intense and reached a crescendo. More wounded were brought in. Cries of agony, terse orders among the staff, and the singing of bone saws filled the air. Nathan was aware of it all, but his attention was fixed on the conversation with the chaplain. They talked through Scriptures he had read all his life but had never paid attention to. The old man explained concepts to Nathan simply and sweetly, pouring water on his thirsty soul. And when the grief came, when the ache of loss for Maria and his brother rose up until he could not speak, the kindly old Swede sat on the cot and held him as he wept.

An orderly came with water. Nathan drank and asked if any others from his company had been brought in. The orderly excused himself and returned shortly with a man who gave Nathan a brief and grim report: over half the company was killed, wounded, or missing, including most of the officers. Captain Shields and Sergeant Jeremiah were among the dead. Nathan thanked him quietly and the man left.

The chaplain rose and put a hand on Nathan's shoulder. "Private, I need to see some of the other men. I will check back on you in time. I leave you in God's hands—the safest place you could possibly be."

"Thank you, sir."

The old man walked off and Nathan lay back on the cot. His head throbbed. He was exhausted. It felt as though every emotion had been drained from him. Despite the sounds of battle in the near distance and the clamor around him, he began to drift off to sleep.

He woke to the sound of his name, on the very edges of his hearing. He began to settle back into sleep, but the sound came again, more insistent, the slightest bit familiar. When he heard his name a third time, very near him, he smiled and reached out a hand. Ezekiel.

"Mister Nathan, bless my soul. It does my heart good to see you, sir." Ezekiel grasped his hand and squeezed it warmly.

"What on earth are you doing here?"

"Well, well, now that's a story and no mistake, Mister Nathan." Ezekiel chuckled. "I'd be happy to tell you presently, but I want to know how you're doin' first. Looks to me like you've gone an' got yourself busted up again."

Nathan was quiet for a bit as thoughts and pictures assembled in his mind. Then slowly he recounted the horrors of the last battle and the encounter with the Confederate soldier. He sighed. "And I may never see again."

Ezekiel said gently, "My heart hurts for you, Mr. Nathan, losin' your brother and all. He stopped for a moment. "As for whether or not your eyes will work again, that part is in God's loving hands."

"I suppose so. But now, tell me how you got here."

Ezekiel leaned back in his seat with the air of an accomplished storyteller and began. It seemed that while the Army of the Potomac had been recovering from the battle of Chancellorsville, Ulysses Grant had led the Army of Tennessee deep into Mississippi. His orders were to capture the fortress city of Vicksburg on the Mississippi River, one of the last points along that mighty waterway still in Confederate hands. Over the next several weeks, he had his troops explore any number of ways to cross to the east bank to bring the city to its knees. Though harassed by Confederate forces through woods and swamps, the army finally crossed with the brave help of Union gunboats and ironclads, and so began a relentless march toward the city.

As the Union troops moved through the countryside, many cotton plantation owners fled in panic, leaving their slaves to fend for themselves. The plantation where Ezekiel's family worked the fields was one such place. His mother and two of his sisters, all that was left by that time, had packed food and a few belongings and left one night. They found other slaves in the woods and only traveled at night, careful to avoid any farms or towns, or soldiers from either side. Eventually, they found help from a volunteer with the Underground Railroad and were guided to its southern hub in North Carolina.

Ezekiel's mother had heard through extended family members on nearby plantations that Ezekiel was a hospital orderly somewhere in Maryland. She asked the Railroad volunteers to send a message ahead to her son that the family was coming north and to look for them in Pennsylvania in the next few weeks. Then she dropped to her knees and implored her Creator to keep her son safe, to see that the message got into his hands, and to guide them on their way.

Ezekiel had received the message less than a week ago. Arrangements were made through the Railroad to meet his family in Harrisburg. A joyous and tearful reunion had taken place in a tanning factory there. The following day Ezekiel heard of the massive forces gathering near Gettysburg. He was assured by Railroad workers that his family would be well looked after. A quick meeting with his mother and sisters ensued in which Ezekiel told them of his obligation to help in the hospitals for the coming battle. He assured them that he would do all in his power to return safely to them as soon as he possibly could. His sisters cried and clung to him. His mother only held his hands briefly and wished him Godspeed. He found a ride with a group of teamsters and arrived at Gettysburg in time to hear Buford's troopers giving the first Confederate divisions a warm reception.

"I came into this tent tonight lookin' for supplies, and I found you."

Nathan sighed and leaned back on the cot. "Ezekiel, that is an amazing story."

"Yessir, certainly is."

"So, what now for you?"

"Well, I imagine I'll keep workin' in the hospitals, as long as they'll have me. I don't think this war is over by a long stretch. And I'll help my family get settled somewhere around these parts." Ezekiel paused for a moment. "But Mr. Nathan, sir, I'm more interested in your story from here."

"How do you mean?"

Ezekiel pulled his chair closer. "Somethin' mighty important has happened to you, Mr. Nathan. You are a different man. I can hear it in your voice."

Nathan raised himself up on his elbows. "What do you hear?" "Freedom, sir, freedom. Some kind of darkness has left you." Tears came to Nathan's eyes.

"And I'll tell you somethin' else, Mr. Nathan. Whatever has happened, I don't believe you're really gonna need your eyes after all. I think the Lord has shown you some things that are beyond human sight. The question is, what will you do with it?" Ezekiel stood and stretched. "Well, sir, I need to be on my way. Plenty of work yet to do."

Nathan reached out a hand and felt Ezekiel take it. "Take care of yourself and your family, Ezekiel. Thank you for coming to see me."

"You take care as well, Mr. Nathan. I pray the good Lord will watch over you and keep showin' you the way to go. Maybe we'll see each other again someday." And with that, he was gone.

Nathan lay back down, suffused with lightness and peace. He reached into a pocket and felt the familiar scrap of paper shaped like a butterfly, given to him so long ago when he had known only darkness and fear. But now . . . a smile slowly spread across his face as tears began to flow once more. Now he could see. For the first time ever in his life, he could see.

ACKNOWLEDGMENTS

IN THIS NOVEL, I have made some effort to be historically accurate (though not exhaustively so), because historical accuracy is important to me, and I wish the story to have integrity.

I wish to acknowledge the following authors from whom I gained valuable information for this book: Edward Rugemen for his article on Charleston, South Carolina Codes for Blacks in the 1840s; Erin Blakemore for her article on the American pupil teacher program in the early 1800s; Eric Foner and John A. Garraty for information from their book *The Readers Companion to American History*, regarding the Kansas Nebraska Act; Allen Ballard for his writing on the Normal School teacher's college; Amanda Onion, Missy Sullivan, and Matt Mullen for their article on the Missouri Compromise; the Lutheran Seminary at Gettysburg, Pennsylvania and their fine website; Manson Parry for his article on Dorothea Dix, in the *American Journal of Public Health*; David Reynolds for his article on the Pottawatomie Massacre; Amanda Onion, Missy Sullivan and Matt Mullen again, for their article on the Dred Scott case; Tony Horwitz for excerpts from his book *Midnight Rising* regarding John Brown at Harper's Ferry; the incomparable Shelby Foote for information from the first book of his seminal trilogy on the Civil War, regarding Fort Sumter; and Andrew Nyr for information from his article on Harewood Hospital in Washington, DC.

As for the senior military and political leaders mentioned in this book, I have attempted to check facts for accuracy on their lives and personalities, though for some events, I have taken at least partial creative license. The main story characters are all fictional, and any similarity in name or description to people living or dead is purely coincidental.